WARNING

This book contains sexually explicit scenes and adult language. It may be considered offensive to some readers. This book is for sale to adults ONLY.

* * * * * * * * * * * * * * * * * * *

Please store your files wisely where they cannot be accessed by underage readers.

ISBN-13: 978-1988083582
ISBN-10: 1988083583

Other Books by Darla Dunbar:

<u>The Romeo Alpha BBW Paranormal Shifter Romance Series</u>

Amanda Walker thinks that she has a normal and boring life. That is until after her 24th birthday. Everything changes when she meets the man who says he was supposed to be her husband. Denying everything the man says, she fights him every step of the way. But after he kidnaps her, Amanda discovers that there are some things about her family that her parents kept a secret all these years. Among the history of the family she learns secrets she thought only happened in story books. Can Amanda tell the difference between truth and lies or is she this mysterious woman that holds the key to a legacy?

<u>Romeo Alpha Blood Lines Romance Series</u>

Twenty-four years have passed in relative peace for Amanda and Romeo. They've raised five children into adulthood and are thoroughly enjoying their lives as the Alpha King and Queen of the werewolves. At twenty-four, Sarina is just stepping into her powers and will be ripe for mating when her birthday comes in two weeks. What no one knows is the danger that lurks just outside their tight knit community. Romeo has made peace with the other clans and has enjoyed that peace, but it will all come crashing down around him when his oldest daughter comes of age to take a mate.

The Alpha Packed BBW Paranormal Shifter Romance Series

Darlene has led a quiet life since suffering through a terrible break-up. She wants nothing more than to spend her time in front of the TV, away from any sort of trouble. But all that goes down the drain when handsome, rugged and rough Idris comes into her life. He is a werewolf on the lookout for his missing pack leader. Darlene quickly finds herself pulled towards this mysterious man and at the same time finds herself falling deeper and deeper into the world of the supernatural.

The Daemon Paranormal Romance Chronicles

The daemon infighting can only be stopped when a strong leader emerges to calm the different factions. Juno appears to be at the heart of the conflict. Things become complicated when Phoebe and Supay try to negotiate with the siren, Juno. The love triangle among Phoebe, Supay and Apollo become tense when Juno's meddling threatens to destroy any romance that develops.

The Mind Talker Paranormal Romance Series

Ananda finds herself on the run and she's not alone. With help from Jared, a stranger that she just met, the two evade capture by an organization that is intent on hunting her kind. Ananda and Jared are able to read minds. When an unfortunate incident happened involving a disturbed individual that resulted in the death of his schoolmates, the secret organization decided to take action.

Valtina is stuck in Middle World, unable to pass on to The Afterlife. In order to redeem herself from past deeds done, she must help bring romance back into the world and stop The Dark Side from destroying love in its entirety. Following orders issued by Ladaya and armed with a leather satchel filled with the appropriate tools and weapons, Valtina embraces each mission with enthusiasm.

Get the latest update on new releases from the author at:

https://darladunbar.com/newsletter/

This book is Part One of the "The Alpha Feud BBW Paranormal Shifter Romance Series"

Book 1

Eliza's life consisted of reporting on boring, crowd-pleasing events, like their country livestock fair. With the arrival of two handsome brothers, the lives of Eliza and her best friend, Melissa, are shaken to the core. For Eliza, the arrival of this new man becomes a test of her relationship with her current boyfriend, who she's been happily living with for over six years. Does Hayden, a complete stranger, really wield the power to make Eliza reconsider her relationship with Andrew?

Book 2

The threat of a new pack arises and the forgiveness of an unintentional murder gives new light to the hearts of all. Among the pain and suffering, the bonds grow deeper, weaving a strong alliance between human and werewolf alike, ready to face the future. Meanwhile, Andrew's true colors come to the surface, leaving Eliza with a difficult choice to make. Does she stay with the man who she has already devoted seven years of her life to or does she choose Hayden, the dark and dangerous stranger, who has stirred the fires of passion within her?

Book 3

Eliza has finally met the man of her dreams and is starting a new life. She is confident that there is nothing in this world that can go wrong. What she doesn't realize is that she isn't in her world anymore. She is in a world surrounded by supernatural beings that she thought only existed in myths. So when both her life and that of her unborn child is threatened by Deimos, an all-powerful supernatural being, she is at odds whether she has been taking her perfect life for granted.

Book 4

Naomi is forced to leave her family to begin her training in Ireland, to replace Deimos as the Wolf Overlord. This brings her to the attention of a great enemy. The enemy has come up with a master plan to break the treaty between hunter and wolf and they will need Naomi to break that treaty. They are planning on using Naomi as their secret weapon against the wolves. How will they get Naomi to agree to all of this? How will they get her to abandon all her morals and beliefs, not to mention her entire family and her friends?

Book 5

Having been fed a poison to forget her life prior to Colt's loving, Naomi struggles to hold onto her faith as he lay in a coma in a hospital. She is greeted by an old friend whom assists her in restoring her previous memories. Following her heart, she trains once more with her masters, getting a unique handle on the ability to transform. She follows her fate that brings her face to face with Deimos. Will her training be enough to defeat and rid the world of Deimos once and for all?

A BBW Paranormal Shifter Romance Series

Alpha Feud

Book One

By Darla Dunbar

Table of Contents

Prologue

"Breaking news: A body has been found in the woods outside the town of Lancaster over the weekend. The county coroner has noted the cause to be what looks like an animal attack.

Sources say there have been sightings of 'wolf-like' creatures found in the area that may or may not be responsible, according to investigators. This is the third unsolved case of this nature that has been reported in the region."

Chapter One

ELIZA TUGGED at the zipper of her wind poncho in an attempt to cover her exposed skin. The wind was getting more fierce and it was still raining, but her network manager believed that rain added to the 'drama' of a broadcast. *Drama? What kind of 'drama' could there possibly be from covering a livestock contest?*

Of course, Eliza would never challenge her boss's choices to his face. Jim was a well-respected man in their town and, in fact, could be regarded as the biggest local celebrity. Jim used to work as an anchor in a major Los Angeles broadcasting station, but had chosen to return to Birkbridge and start his own broadcasting company. They had started off small but had managed to accumulate a decent following of loyal viewers and had therefore been able to expand into a full-fledged TV and radio station.

Under Jim's influence, Eliza had lived for a long time in a state of bedazzlement. After all, she had, once upon a time, fallen in love with the world of Jim's creation. Jim and his television station - Birkbridge NewsLine - had brought some sense of excitement to the otherwise boring little town. The problem was that, after five years of working for the man, she'd learned to see through the sparkly shades of spectacle. Once the illusion had shattered, the outcome was quite depressing; Eliza was, once more, living in the real world.

For people like Eliza's boyfriend, Andrew Freelander, 'normal' was not synonymous with boring. He was a man of simple pleasures and routine; he enjoyed his black coffee in the mornings and his beers in the evenings. Every other day, he went to shoot some pool at the local pub with his friends and colleagues from the weapons factory. Sometimes Eliza joined, sometimes she didn't. She didn't plan ahead most of the time, because she didn't want her entire life to be dominated by routine. Thanks to Jim, she felt as if her life might change for a while and become at least a little less monotonous. However, after many years, Eliza's new and 'exciting' life became its own routine.

And at the moment, she stood in front of a farm, reporting on an upcoming livestock show in the pouring rain. *Yippidy yay.*

"And now, reporting from the Birkbridge countryside farm: a soaked and very cold cow!" Eliza shouted into the camera.

Oliver, the cameraman, rolled his eyes. "Thank God we're not filming live television!" he yelled at her through the roaring wind. "And I don't see any cows around here, but I'm so bloody tired of not doing my job today that I might just be hallucinating!"

The wind was finally dying down and Oliver was pointing his camera at Eliza again. "None of that "cow" nonsense this time, Eliza! The people of this town are paying good money to get their news from a real human woman."

"You make a good point." Eliza smiled. Oliver was a good sport; he was the only British person in Birkbridge, and he certainly knew how to have a good bit of banter. Eliza decided to cut him some slack and snap into work mode; she knew that the rain might start again in a few seconds so they needed to get the shot right then and there.

"This is Eliza Zachary, reporting from the soon-to-be Birkbridge livestock fair. As you can see, preparations are under way for the upcoming festivities…"

Whenever she did stories like this, Eliza couldn't help but wonder what it would've been like if she'd accepted the job offer in Boston. The job had initially seemed way beyond her reach, but her father had pulled some strings with a few of his contacts at the news station and managed to convince Eliza to apply. To her amazement, she had been immediately accepted for the role of an on-site broadcasting journalist. Pursuing the job in Boston would have allowed Eliza to do what she'd always wanted and follow in the footsteps of her father. Granted, she wouldn't be on any real battlefront, but she would still be in the position to make history with her news stories. However, taking the job in Boston would also have prevented her from continuing her happy life with Andrew, her loving, loyal boyfriend.

Andrew and Eliza first met in their first year of college and had been inseparable ever since. She believed that Andrew was the only person, other than her dad, who she could truly be herself around. Although they didn't exactly have an instant connection, Eliza and Andrew grew close in a very natural way, and their relationship developed with ease. Before starting her first year of Media Studies, Eliza had promised herself that she would make an effort to interact with other people. College was meant to be the best time of her life, and Eliza wasn't about to let her insecurities get in the way of that. With some life coaching and advice from her dad and some styling tips from her mom, Eliza had fashioned her very own alter ego with which she would face the world head-on.

Through thick and thin, Eliza's father had always been her rock. Her mother, Jeanette, was always supportive, but she was sometimes a bit too fussy for Eliza to truly confide in her.

While growing up, Eliza had known her father as two men: the brave, effortlessly cool man who yelled over the sound of gunfire from the television screen, and the reserved, gentle man who tucked her into bed every night. Of course, the television Martin looked a lot different, since Eliza watched all his broadcasts as old recordings. By the time she was born, Martin had given up his career and settled down in Birkbridge to raise his family. He became a local historian, pursuing lengthy and in-depth projects relating to the foundational elements of Birkbridge life. These revolved around the three main industries in the town: coal-mining, farming and manufacturing guns. His new book required him to research the inner workings of the Millstone Firearms factory, and he could often be found hanging out in the area, talking to some of the workers. Some of the workers didn't mind him, but others would sneer at him and ask him condescending questions. "Have you ever tried using Google, old man? You know we don't have all day to chat with you about your picture books."

Despite his seemingly old-fashioned methods and even though he was a bit of a social outcast, Martin was still unbelievably charming. Perhaps it was due to his immaculately well-preserved good looks, or maybe because of his patience and open-minded listening skills, but Martin's investigative projects usually bore fantastic results. He often took on paid projects for some extra cash. Sometimes, locals would hire him to investigate and produce their family trees. In other cases, his clients were people who wanted him to find anecdotes or even write entire biographies for their dead relatives' funerals. One thing was for sure; his clients were never disappointed.

Going along with her father's suggestion, Eliza joined the drama club and after five months, Eliza had had a decent amount of interaction with the club's one and only groupie; a cute senior named Andrew. At first, she was a little annoyed with his tendency to hang around and watch their practices. Eliza was new to this scene and still felt a bit self-conscious, particularly around people who weren't even part of the theater group. For this reason, Andrew's casual presence had frustrated her a little bit. Who was this guy? Didn't he have anything better to do?

The first time that Eliza found herself alone with Andrew, she had been unexpectedly upfront with him. She was usually shy around guys, but she found him so *annoying* that her frustration managed to surpass her bashfulness. Although sarcasm hadn't been part of her repertoire at the time, Eliza's first conversation with Andrew was loaded with it.

"Haven't seen you in a while," she'd said with a cheeky grin on her face. "You must've been real busy lately."

Andrew had been at their practices every single day that week, so he laughed at her ironic insinuations that he had no life. And, as it turned out, Andrew had liked Eliza's direct approach to conversation. Due to her former friendlessness, Eliza hadn't really learned how to engage in small talk and empty chitchat; she was an all-or-nothing kind of girl. Andrew, as an attractive college senior, had become accustomed to empty, flirtatious interactions with the opposite sex. However, Andrew was a self-proclaimed monogamist and he quickly tired of the attention overload. Throughout college, he'd been looking to settle down, but to his dismay, all the co-eds seemed the same to him; he never found anyone amongst his groupies who really challenged him the right way. So Andrew became a groupie himself and started hanging out with the drama club. As he explained to Eliza, he was looking to find some truth in the fiction of theater. Eliza had rolled her eyes and called him a cheeseball. Then they exchanged looks, Eliza's mouth twisting into a crooked smile, and they both burst into laughter.

Andrew had been persistent, and had won Eliza over within two weeks. They'd hang out after the theater club practices, and their private meetings had escalated. At first, they met up in cafés, then bars, and eventually, Andrew's apartment. Quickly, Eliza and Andrew became in sync with one another, and there was no awkwardness in discussing their plans for the future. After she completed her sophomore year, Andrew asked Eliza to move in with him, and she gladly accepted.

Andrew had graduated three years earlier than Eliza and immediately got a job at Millstone Firearms. After five years his responsibilities had increased immensely. Despite his reputation for being late to almost everything, Andrew was nothing but exceptional at what he did, in fact, ever since Andrew received his promotion to junior head of sales, Millstone Firearms had managed to out-sell their competitors by ten percent annually, which meant that they were finally on their way to becoming the most successful firearms manufacturer in the country.

For Eliza, parting with Andrew hadn't really been an option. Since she hadn't, in her wildest dreams, expected that the Boston network would actually consider her application, let alone offer her a job, Eliza had been completely befuddled about how to act when she'd received the offer. Deep down, she had already known that Andrew would not be willing to give up his job and leave Birkbridge, and she also realized that he simply wouldn't be able to keep up with the pace of life in the east coast. After all, the only things that kept Andrew's absent-mindedness at bay were his routines and habits, but he was completely unable to adjust to changes in his schedule.

Nevertheless, Eliza had had a tiny speckle of hope when she confronted Andrew about her job offer. He had been incredibly sweet, kissing Eliza and telling her that he was so proud of her; after all, what were the odds for getting such an incredible job offer straight-out-of-college? However, the fantasy wasn't meant to last. After lengthy conversations over breakfast, dinner and weekend pillow talk, Andrew and Eliza eventually came to the sad yet inevitable conclusion that the move to Boston wasn't going to pan out. They both knew that Andrew had worked incredibly hard to achieve his current company status, and neither of them believed that he should have to start from square one again. They discussed the possibility of Eliza moving on her own, but her fully packed Boston work schedule would ultimately overrule the possibility of her flying out to see Andrew once every few months. For Andrew, given his recent promotion, the chances of taking time for visitation days were also very slim.

As Eliza helped Oliver pack up his camera equipment, she told herself that she had no regrets. In actuality, the decision to stay in Birkbridge with Andrew had been a no-brainer. She had been able to get everything she wanted: a loving boyfriend *and* a job. Granted, this job may not have been a first choice, but it was certainly not a job that anyone in their right mind could complain about.

Arriving home, Eliza checked the time on her phone, 6:29 pm, and in the process discovered several texts from Melissa, one of her three best friends and also, coincidentally, a cousin.

5:30: *Done with work, where are you right now?*

5:44: *Not gonna bother going home first, brought a change of clothes to work so heading to the bar now! Will see you there.*

6:08: *There's a hot guy here. Hurry or I'll go home with him!*

6:10: *Just kidding but seriously, get here already.*

When Eliza walked into *Nelly's*, Melissa was sitting at their usual spot. There were a few empty glasses already lined up at the table, but she was still looking relatively sharp. As Eliza knew from experience, Melissa could be trusted to hold her liquor. Even on nights when she consumed triple the doses of her friends, Melissa would always be the last one standing.

Eliza took a seat opposite her friend. "So where's this dreamy guy? I was almost expecting you to be gone by the time I arrived."

"All kidding aside, if my vodka-goggles aren't deceiving me, I think there really *is* a somewhat hot guy here tonight. He's at the bar though, so be a doll and check him out for me while you're up there?"

Eliza rolled her eyes and sighed dramatically, but she couldn't stop herself from smiling. "Oh, all right then. But only because I love you."

"You're the best!" Melissa beamed, giving her friend an overly exaggerated wink. There was something about their weekly girly meet-ups that had spurred the friends to engage in a satirical 80's-housewife-routine.

Eliza came back from the bar, carrying two cocktails. "So, no sight of Brienne yet. Or has she also wondered off with some mystery man?"

"Yes. She's finally left boring old Tom and those dreadful kids and found herself a real man," Melissa responded, without breaking character.

At that moment, Brienne came through the door, dithering about as always. She wiped her feet on the carpet and, spotting the flaw of their seating arrangement, shuffled over to another table and grabbed a chair.

"Hey, sorry I'm so late, what did I miss?"

"Not much. Well, Melissa has spotted someone she thinks is hot, but that's about it," Eliza responded matter-of-factly.

"Ah, good, so I didn't miss anything," Brienne confirmed, slouching back on her chair and looking calm at last.

Chapter Two

A few hours and many drinks later, Eliza, Melissa and Brienne were still at the bar, cackling and giggling like schoolgirls, talking about boys, reminiscent of their old slumber party days.

"Why has that guy two tables away been staring at you all night?" Melissa said in a conspiring whisper to Brienne.

Eliza and Brienne turned to Melissa, both looking a bit surprised.

"Which guy?"

"That guy to your left – two tables away. He's sitting with his hat-wearing friend. You can't see him properly from where you're facing, but I could see him all night. And he kept looking at you, Brienne."

Eliza's head instinctively started turning toward the guy.

"Eliza! Stop, you're being obvious," Brienne whispered bashfully.

As she watched the other two fuss about, a smile broke out on Melissa's face. "It's fine, what's the harm in looking? He's been looking over here all night. Eliza, turn back and let Brienne look."

Brienne stretched back in her chair and spun her body to the left, pulling up her arms in an exaggerated sigh. She turned back swiftly.

"I think we made eye contact," she whispered anxiously.

Melissa and Eliza burst into a fit of giggles.

After looking at the other two for a few seconds, Brienne burst into laughter as well. Eliza realized that she was having a lot of fun. As the giggles died down, she returned to reality and began to realize how unique her friends were. Only they could create an exciting night out of a seemingly empty, uneventful night at the local pub.

Eliza noticed that Brienne's mood had changed drastically from exasperated to genuinely relaxed and joyful. She wasn't sure whether the man from a few tables away had really been staring at Brienne, or whether Melissa had said so to soothe Brienne's looming insecurities. Whatever the truth may have been, the story had significantly lifted Brienne's spirits, which is all that mattered. And at the end of the day, that's what friends were for; to know exactly what their friends needed before they realized it themselves.

Smiling, Brienne looked at her phone. It was nearly eleven. "I think I've had all the excitement that an old party pooper like me can handle for one night," she laughed.

"Oh, that's not true! Plenty more excitement is on its way!" Melissa responded enthusiastically.

"I really should be getting home now. But you guys stay, enjoy your night, don't let it be ruined – not by me, not by anybody!"

"Oh all right then, come here you." Eliza stretched out her arms for a hug.

"Same time next week?"

"You betcha. And if you're late again, you're buying the next round. This goes for all of us, by the way," Melissa added, lifting her eyebrow indicatively at Eliza.

After Brienne left, Melissa went to the bar to get a round. Eliza was halfway through writing a text to Andrew, when suddenly she heard Melissa sit back down and utter what sounded like a high-pitched squeal.

"He talked to me," she half-shrieked, half-whispered.

"Who?"

"Who do you think? The hot guy!"

"Oh!"

"He said he's coming over!"

Eliza turned to the bar subtly, attempting to decipher what was going on. "What exactly did he say to you?"

"He said he thought I looked 'stunning'. Yep, he actually used that word, and then he said he's coming over and he's going to get 'me and my lovely friend' a drink!"

Eliza nodded enthusiastically and voiced her approval, but deep down she couldn't help but feel mildly uncomfortable. If Brienne hadn't left, it would've been a bit less awkward, but at this point she was already preparing to be the third wheel. This wouldn't be the first time that she'd gotten a drink from a guy purely out of being associated with Melissa. Even though it stung a little to witness guys flirting with her friend, Eliza always put on a brave face. After all, Eliza was the one with the boyfriend, and she would do everything to make her friend's dating life a little less tragic. After all, it wasn't Melissa's fault that their town was so small.

"All the good ones are taken, and if not, they're my exes!" Melissa had complained on numerous occasions. She made a good point.

The man was walking over, two drinks in hand. Eliza couldn't help but stare; this man was gorgeous, almost too perfect. And he seemed to be neither taken *nor* an ex of Melissa's. Eliza pushed away the twinge of envy and discovered genuine happiness for her friend lurking beyond the surface. This might actually *be* something!

"Hi, nice to see you again," he said to Melissa, his words formal but his voice bordering on cheeky. He turned to Eliza. "Your friend has told me that you come here every week, is that true?"

Eliza blinked, slightly stunned. She realized that a moment had passed and she hadn't said anything, so she forced her voice into action. "Uh, yeah, it's just a thing we do. We decided that it helps to set a time and a place for our catch-ups. Plus they have good beer here."

The man smiled dreamily and chuckled. Eliza blushed.

"I'm Theo. It's very nice to meet you." He smiled and placed one drink in front of Eliza, and the other in front of Melissa.

Melissa was beaming from ear to ear. "Thanks!"

"It's my pleasure," said Theo, occupying Brienne's vacant seat.

Chapter Three

The following day, Eliza was scheduled to cover the first day of the livestock fair, which was to begin at two in the afternoon. Considering that she stayed up late the night before, she had a bit of a lie-in. Since she was running around to different locations for the majority of her waking days, Eliza really cherished free mornings such as this.

After she got out of bed, she went to the kitchen and cooked herself up a filling, balanced breakfast. Instead of her usual routine of cereal bars somewhere between her car and the office, Eliza decided to really take her time with cooking. She even made a smoothie and found an old show to watch on Netflix while eating. If there was even a slight hint of a hangover when she woke up, the breakfast had certainly cured the remainder of it. Eliza concentrated on the TV show and tried not to let her thoughts linger on the previous night, which had turned out to be a little bizarre.

There was just something about this Theo that didn't quite sit right with Eliza. She had always known Melissa to be anything but a cheap drunk. Melissa was very good at holding her alcohol and yet last night she had somehow gotten really tipsy really fast. Something about it just didn't seem right.

Sure, Theo had volunteered to help Melissa to the car and losing the fight over who should be taking Melissa home. Eliza couldn't help but notice the way he looked at her as he was helping her into the car. He looked at her as if she was a meal, like he was hungry. Eliza just wasn't sure if it was a sexual hunger or something else.

Although Melissa's drunkenness was completely understandable, given the cumulative amount of drinks she'd consumed throughout the night, Eliza still couldn't shake a feeling that something was off. *Not all men are rapists. And even if Theo were a creep, why would he have to drug anybody? With that face and those shoulders, he could have anyone he wanted.* He looked like a model straight out of a sports magazine. He was all tan, with nothing but muscle, and his chocolate brown hair hung just below his eye, brushing his perfectly sculpted cheek bones. His eyes were something else too. They were a soft shade of green with little flecks of gold in them. Plus, he was tall, so, so tall.

However, it hadn't been the circumstances that bothered Eliza so much as a feeling she got when she looked at Theo.

I'm reading way too much into this. I'm feeling pretty tipsy as well.

Three episodes of *Friends* later, Eliza took a long, luxurious shower. She brushed her hair and towel dried it, before proceeding to brush it all over again. Her hair had always been the most time-consuming aspect of her routine. Eliza's hair was long, dark and naturally wavy, but if she didn't style it, it would turn into a ball of frizz and knots. After combing it thoroughly, she picked up a round brush and a hair dryer and began the laborious process of shaping her locks into beautiful curls. She finished off the look with a few spritzes of anti-frizz hairspray.

By 11:30, Eliza began to feel a little bored. She wasn't used to having free alone time and couldn't help but feel a little antsy. Perhaps the events of the night before were still weighing a little bit on her subconscious. To alleviate her need for doing stuff, Eliza decided that she would bring Andrew some lunch. She rarely got to see him during the workdays, and even though they used to sometimes meet at 12:30 for coffee and sandwiches, Andrew's promotion had brought him new responsibilities that overruled any lunch date opportunities so Eliza assembled a pretty magnificent looking sandwich, using some leftover turkey from dinner and piling on an array of condiments, veggies and cheese. She wrapped it up in foil, grabbed a can of iced tea from the fridge, and stuffed the contents into her handbag.

Twenty minutes later, Eliza pulled up outside of the Millstone Firearms factory. This had been the workplace of Andrew's father, and his grandfather, and possibly even his great-grandfather. Eliza sometimes zoned out a little during the family tree conversations, which were a tad too common during Thanksgiving dinner. The factory and office buildings merged together, and the result was a colossal structure of pretty epic proportions. To outsiders, it may have seemed that Birkbridge was built around this factory, but as Eliza's third grade history teacher had taught them, this was not the case. Birkbridge, Indiana was actually an old mining town, and coal continued to be the town's main export, alongside agricultural and livestock outputs.

Eliza flashed her visitor badge and took the elevator to the fifteenth floor. Even though she'd been over to visit Andrew a few times before, she still experienced feelings of surprise and awe whenever she walked into his executive office. Andrew's secretary was away, so she decided to just let herself in. Her boyfriend was staring into his laptop, deep in thought, and didn't seem to hear the door open.

"Hey," Eliza said, smiling.

Andrew looked up from his computer, his expression changing instantly. "Oh hey there, baby!" He looked genuinely thrilled to see her, and this gave Eliza butterflies in her stomach. When she got home the night before, Andrew had already been asleep, and he'd woken up in the morning before she did. The moment he looked up into her eyes, flashing his winning golden-boy smile, she realized that nothing else should matter. Why had she been so concerned about looking attractive to men in bars when she had Andrew? Perhaps it was just easy to take people for granted when you saw them every day.

"Don't they give you lunch breaks around here?" Eliza teased.

"Nope, they've got us slaving away all day, daydreaming about tasty meals and cold beers…"

"I see, it's all part of their mind games. Hungry workers are obedient workers."

"That's right. God, you're smart. Come over here." Andrew stretched out his arms and closed his eyes. Eliza strolled up to his desk and placed the sandwich bag into one of his outstretched hands. Andrew opened his eyes.

"Is this? Nooo, oh my God, you are seriously the best thing ever."

Andrew proceeded to shovel the contents of the bag into his mouth, gulping down the food like air.

"I hadn't realized that mankind had developed the ability to *inhale* food, but I guess you're just one step ahead of me in the chain of human evolution," Eliza said matter-of-factly.

"That could be one explanation, but a more plausible reason for my gluttony is the fact that I'm actually ridiculously low down in the human evolution chain. You've seen how secluded my family is; we're like a surviving population of Neanderthals."

"Mmm… I love my Neanderthal man."

"And I love my sexy girlfriend who makes me amazing turkey sandwiches." Andrew took another bite. "Wow, is that pickle I taste?"

"Sure is."

"Nice. Who would've even known that pickle could taste so *good* with turkey?"

"I guess there're many things that Neanderthal men have yet to learn."

Eliza had an hour left before she needed to return to the livestock fair, so she hung out in the office with Andrew. At first, they chatted a little bit about their plans to re-paint their house. They'd made the big move out of Andrew's old apartment and into their current place only three months ago, and there was still a lot of work to be done. They wanted to paint the exterior and add an additional bathroom upstairs. They made a promise to make arrangements with the painters and the construction workers tomorrow. Eliza kissed Andrew on the mouth and nibbled at his neck. He pinched her butt and she yelped, jumping backward and laughing.

They caught up about the day before, and Eliza told him about Melissa's sudden drunkenness. She told him about Theo, but decided not to mention her odd suspicions. After all, she had no basis for any of her paranoid thoughts, so she decided not to burden her boyfriend with this unnecessary information.

Andrew had laughed at the story, but Eliza detected a hint of pity for Melissa. Throughout his entire life, Andrew had been a one-woman man, and he strongly believed in the notion of settling down with the person you love and staying with them for life. Eliza was incredibly grateful that she could trust him to be faithful, but she sometimes thought that he oversimplified human relationships. Perhaps this was a hangover from his childhood, since he had been lucky enough to witness successful thriving marriages.

Even now, Eliza couldn't name a single failed relationship amongst his many cousins. Perhaps people really did take after their parents in more ways than they let themselves believe. For Eliza, it was difficult to determine whether or not her parents' relationship had affected her. In theory, Jeanette and Martin were still married and living together, but she was aware that they didn't share the same bed. Her mother had always been a little bit insecure and seemed to never have gotten over her outsider status. Nowadays, her father had also become somewhat of an outsider in their town. Although this should've brought her parents closer together, it seemed to have the opposite effect. The more her father retreated into his world of history and research, the more insecure and distant her mother would become. This, ultimately, would push her father away even more, and thus began the vicious cycle.

Eliza witnessed how her mother's insecurities had blossomed throughout her marriage to an attractive semi-celebrity, and sincerely hoped that this wasn't a window into her future with Andrew. She certainly hoped that they would turn out like his parents, but she knew that Andrew was wary of being like his parents, too. It seemed that they were destined for their own path; the two of them against the world. In many ways, this was a comforting thought.

Andrew was drinking his iced tea and leaning his feet against his desk counter. Eliza had taken his place at the main desk and was feeling powerful. They were in the middle of a heated discussion.

"No, sweetie, I'm not even complaining, I'm just *saying* that we used to not cover this kind of crap. I'm just worried for Jim, that's all. He might be losing his flair," Eliza continued.

"I'm sure he'll find a way to make it interesting, El. People watch Jim's channel for the same reason they buy Millstone guns; they want to experience something that combines the Midwestern experience with an air of sophistication and excitement."

"And what exactly is the Midwestern experience? Shooting things and gazing at cow dung?"

"Yeah, that's pretty much it," Andrew laughed.

"Well, where's the sophistication and excitement then?"

"Excitement doesn't have to be about seeing something new. Everything on TV is pushing the envelope so much these days, and people eventually become desensitized by it. What they really want to see is something relatable. The excitement comes from the fact that they see you on TV, standing at a place that's accessible for them. When they go to the livestock fair, they can feel special because they're going to a place that they saw on television."

"Hmm. I might not completely agree with you, but you sure are a great salesman," Eliza admitted.

"Damn right I am!" Andrew chuckled.

Eliza's broadcast went pretty well that afternoon, but she was glad to get home when it was over. She was looking forward to a quiet night in with Andrew, when her phone began to ring. *Oh no… don't answer it.* Eliza checked the phone and it was Melissa. She hadn't spoken to her since she'd brought her home the night before, so she was pretty concerned about her friend's wellbeing. She picked up the phone on the second ring.

"Hey, Melissa, are you ok?"

"Hey, yeah, of course I'm fine! Are you?" Melissa replied briskly.

Eliza was unsure whether Melissa's tone had been defensive or whether she genuinely didn't realize she had been that drunk. "Yeah, I'm good, I'm just asking because you were a little… I mean, we were all a bit tipsy last night, but you were especially tipsy. Not in a bad way or anything, just wanted to make sure you were ok."

"Yeah, of course. Sorry if I was acting loopy, guess I haven't been out in a while! Anyway, sorry about being so last minute, but I wanted to ask you a huge favor."

Chapter Four

"Sure, what is it?" asked Eliza.

"Well," Melissa stalled, "I hope this is ok, but I kind of told the guy from last night, Theo, that we'd go on a double date with him tonight."

"*We?*"

"Yeah, I mean me, you and Andrew."

There was a pause.

"Well, I guess we don't have a choice now, because you already said we'd go!" Eliza replied, unable to hide her frustration. *When did Melissa speak to Theo? I didn't even realize they'd exchanged numbers!*

"Melissa, I don't mind going out with you guys, but you know Andrew, he's a man of routine. Plus, he has to get up really early tomorrow morning. I doubt he'll be able to stay out late."

Melissa seemed to perk up. "That's totally fine, just ask him to come out for a couple of drinks, that's all!"

"Ok, I'll call you back."

Eliza hung up, slouched back on her couch and sighed. She knew Andrew wouldn't like this, and she was certainly not thrilled. *Why couldn't Melissa have just asked before making plans?* Despite her reservations, she still wanted to be a good friend, and Eliza would prefer to tag along rather than let Melissa go off alone with this strange man. Not that she still thought that he'd tried to drug her, but perhaps her suspicions were justified by the fact that strangers were simply *rare* in their town, and it was therefore simply harder to trust them.

Andrew reluctantly agreed to come along, on the condition that he could leave as early as eight. Eliza sent him text-message appreciation kisses and assured him that he was free to go as soon as he wanted, as long as he just showed his face at the restaurant.

Eliza drove up to the restaurant and met Andrew in the parking lot. They shared a kiss and a cigarette, which Eliza enjoyed even though she didn't consider herself to be a smoker. Andrew used to not be one either, but ever since he'd gotten his own office, it had seemed as if he was running a one-man cigar club. Apparently, part of the Millstone Firearms image involved being a "manly man", and Andrew had to project that image while meeting with clients. Despite the macho talk, Eliza knew that smoking was less of a pleasure than a weakness. She usually hated smelling smoke on her boyfriend when he came home from work, but today was an exception. After smelling cow dung all day at the livestock fair, Eliza felt that she could use the cigarette.

Eliza and Andrew were a few minutes late, however, Eliza couldn't spot Melissa's car in the parking lot either. They were the first of their party to arrive. Andrew went ahead and ordered food, since he knew that he would have to dash off before the rest. About fifteen minutes later, Melissa arrived, looking beautiful but flustered, and possibly a little tipsy.

"Hey, sorry I'm late. Is he here?"

"Nope, so I guess that makes two of you!" Eliza replied, trying to lighten the mood. She knew that Melissa would be concerned about Theo's tardiness. In order to distract her friend from pondering the possibility that she was stood up by her date, she decided to appeal to her baser instincts. "Drinks?"

"Sounds good to me."

Melissa sat down, looking slightly more upbeat after Eliza's proposition. However, she had a look of worry in her eyes that made Eliza question her friend's state of mind.

"Hey, is everything ok with you?"

"Yes," Melissa responded, staring up into space for a second. "Well, actually no," she hesitated. "It's all ok now, but I had to go see my mom, and it was a little so-so with her, but I think she's calmed down a bit. But I was worried I'd be late, and you two would be stuck here with my date all this time, but as it turns out that didn't happen so I'm pretty glad!"

"What happened with your mother?" Andrew asked gently.

Melissa looked thoughtful again. "It turned out that nothing had really *happened*, but she called me earlier today and there was something about the way she *sounded* that scared the daylights out of me. I'm not sure what was on my mind, maybe I just got paranoid over nothing. I drove over and got stuck in traffic, so I called her from the car and she wasn't picking up. So I called one of the nurses and she went to check on her, and assured me that everything was fine. I finally arrived at the hospital to find that she was fine, indeed."

"So she wasn't sick or anything? It was just a false alarm?" Eliza inquired.

"Not exactly. She wasn't sick or feeling ill physically, but she began spewing some nonsense. It wasn't anything malicious but… I don't know how to explain it, it upset me a little."

"What did she say?" Eliza inquired as she fidgeted nervously with her straw.

"She… uh, well, it's stupid." Melissa blinked her eyes rapidly to prevent herself from tearing up. "She started yapping about how I was about to make a big mistake, and she had a dream, and she didn't tell me what happened in the dream but she just flat-out told me that I should cancel all my plans tonight and lock myself in the house. She told me that something bad was going to happen to me, but didn't tell me why or when."

"What did you say?"

"What *could* I say? This was utter nonsense, even for my mother. This 'something bad is going to happen' thing is just a way for her to say 'I don't trust you with making your own life decisions,' and it's infuriating! I'm a grown woman, and the only reason that I'm still in this dingy hole of a town is because of *her*."

Melissa took a breath and it appeared as if a demon left her body. Her eyes flittered from rage to compassion, and she looked up at Andrew and Eliza apologetically.

"Shit, guys, I'm sorry, I didn't really mean that. There's nothing wrong with this town, it's *me* that's all wrong. It's just that too much has *happened* here already that I feel the need to move on with my life, but I can't. And when I began thinking that I'd screwed up my chances for meeting a new man, then bang, I suddenly meet a hot stranger at the bar the other day. Just like that! And then my mother almost screws it up for me by making me drive to her loony bin… I mean her care hospital, and almost making me miss the date. Speaking of which, what is taking him so long?"

Just as she uttered those words, Eliza noticed a perfectly shaped figure walking through the door.

"Speak of the devil," she said.

Theo walked over with a smile on his face, but his eyes were looking tired. Even though he looked devastatingly handsome, there was still something about his appearance that suggested he hadn't slept that night.

Melissa turned to her date and smiled with genuine gratitude. Eliza realized how much she must appreciate his company right now.

Eliza had met Naomi, Melissa's mother, sixteen years ago, when Naomi had been at her peak, both in beauty and in charm. However, due to a decline in her mental state, Naomi hadn't spoken to any of her former friends or family members in the past ten years. In actuality, Melissa and Eliza's families were intertwined, since Eliza's father was Naomi's cousin. However, the girls had met at school and had been completely unaware of their familial relation until they were surprised by this information at a mutual aunt's wedding ceremony.

The saddest thing about Naomi's mental health issues was the lack of support that she received from her community. Throughout her life, she had never had that many people on her side. The curse of good looks seemed to be prevalent in their family, since just like Eliza's father, Naomi had been scorned by many citizens of Birkbridge as a result of her attractiveness. To make matters worse, Naomi was a single mother, who had never been married, which spurred malicious rumors about the nature of her profession and private life. Many believed that a desperate woman would go through many lengths just to support the wellbeing of her only child.

Many of the hateful, jealous people who took pleasure in shunning Naomi from the social circles of Birkbridge had made accusations that she was 'unhinged', 'godless' and 'crazy'. Due to the irony of fate, or perhaps thanks to the destructive powers of psychological bullying, things had taken a turn for the worse and Naomi ended up in a mental care unit.

Public opinion about the woman had recently changed from scorn to pity. Finally, the citizens of Birkbridge had begun to feel guilty about the way they treated her, since they were confronted with the plight of Naomi's daughter. Melissa was a very outgoing member of the community, which possibly resulted from her eagerness to please people to avoid ending up like her mother. It was no secret that Melissa had been the only person to help her mother during the darkest of times while the latter descended into madness. Prior to her final retreat to the mental hospital, Naomi had been the talk of the town on several occasions.

The first incident occurred when a jewelry store clerk arrived at six in the morning to open up the store for business, and had found Naomi lying there, asleep on the floor. After a thorough investigation, the police declared that nothing had been stolen or moved, and after a few hours of interrogation at the police station, Naomi was set free.

There was another time, when she was found stumbling out of an abandoned building. This happened a couple more times, in equally bizarre locations and under similarly odd circumstances. And every single time, the story was the same. She didn't remember why she was there or how she had gotten there, and no evidence was present to support claims of 'breaking and entering', since there was no damage to the property. During this time, the prostitution rumors were even more rampant. However, after a while, people began to show some genuine concern at last. It was almost as if they had wanted Naomi to be crazy all along, and now that she was, they were suddenly able to accept her.

Nowadays, the only information that Eliza ever received about her second aunt was through Melissa, and Melissa didn't really like to talk about her mother. Of course, Eliza made sure to never push her friend beyond her comfort zone in regards to this delicate issue, but she nevertheless made sure to inquire about her wellbeing from time to time.

For the past year, there seemed to have been very little wrong with Naomi, and Melissa had begun to fear that social isolation was actually preventing her recovery. The nurses had even confirmed that Naomi was well enough to come back and live at home with Melissa, but Naomi seemed reluctant to move back. Melissa had still been hopeful that her mother would come around, but now things seemed to be taking a turn in a negative direction. Even though today's episode didn't seem like a big deal, the minor anxiety attack could still be symptomatic of wider mental issues. Of course, Eliza hoped that this wasn't the case, and she sincerely wished the best for her best friend and her mother. She certainly hoped that Melissa would have a good time with Theo and forget all about what had happened.

Despite the initial awkwardness caused by Theo's late arrival, the mood had picked up. By the time the second round of drinks was served, the conversation was flowing with relative ease. Andrew and Theo seemed to be getting along fine, even though they were disagreeing about almost everything. In fact, the two seemed like the polar opposites of one another, with only the exception of their good looks and charm. However, they were both attractive in completely different ways. Andrew was a strawberry blonde suburban boy, with stubble on his face and a dimple on his left cheek. He was irresistibly handsome in a kind of man-child way, since his physique was broad and muscular, but his eyes had a glint of child-like *joie de vivre*. He was a man who could appreciate the same things over and over again; his food, his beer, his job, his friends, and, of course, his beloved girlfriend.

On the other side of the spectrum, there was Theo; a dark-haired man with a body made for business attire, perfectly symmetrical face and cheekbones that could slice through glass. His eyes were that of an adrenaline junkie. Unlike the routine-loving Andrew, Theo seemed to be the type of man who would do almost anything to chase after a new experience. Nevertheless, his manners were calm and gentlemanly, and his flirtation seemed pretty under control. Even so, Eliza suspected that this man had plenty of experience with the ladies. As he talked about his many travels, she couldn't help but wonder whether he went from town to town, sweeping women off their feet, only to leave them for the next.

Even if he were a womanizer, she wouldn't dream of interfering with Melissa's life, since if there was anything that Melissa *hated*, it was being told what to do. Nevertheless, Eliza hoped that she was wrong about this man and that there was some possible future there for her friend. Melissa deserved more than just the string of one-night stands that had made her weary over the past few years.

By the time that the main courses arrived, Andrew had already finished his dinner, since he had ordered prior to the arrival of Melissa and Theo. He excused himself, gave Eliza a tender kiss on the lips and headed out of the door.

The others ordered another round of drinks and toasted.

"To new friendships," Theo said, giving Melissa a cheeky wink.

Melissa giggled whole-heartedly. The flirtation between her and Theo had escalated throughout the night and she seemed to be having a really good time.

"Since it's only 8:30, would the two of you like to go to the bar? I haven't been there on a Friday night but I hear it's worth experiencing," Theo suggested. His voice and manner was still suave as ever, the alcohol not seeming to have affected him.

"I'd love to go," Melissa responded without batting an eyelid.

Eliza looked over at Melissa awkwardly, since she was about to make her excuses and go home. But now that Melissa had agreed to go, she didn't want to sully the moment. They made eye contact and Eliza managed to deliver the message without opening her mouth.

"I'll be right back, just going to the restroom," Eliza said.

"I'll come with," Melissa chimed in.

As soon as they were outside of earshot, Eliza began to jabber. "I really want to come out with the two of you, but Andrew's already gone home and he expects that I'll be back after dinner."

"El, you've been really really sweet with me today, and I know that I sort of made you come here without even getting your consent first. And I haven't even had the chance to thank you for that, but trust me, I will. I owe you one, big time. But you realize that after the day that I've had, I don't feel right going off with Theo on my own. It's not that I don't trust him, but I barely know him." Her voice lightened, and she smiled up at Eliza. "And, let's face it, I would like to prove my mother wrong and show that I *am* a responsible human being!"

Eliza smiled back. She thought about Melissa's mother again and felt a pang of guilt for wanting to ditch her friend at a time like this.

"Oh, all right then. I'll come along. But just for one drink!"

"One. Not a drop more, I promise! You're the best, El, seriously, words can't even express how cool you've been. All I can say is that Andrew is one heck of a lucky bastard."

Eliza smiled coyly, waving her arm as if to dismiss the shower of compliments. She put her arm around Melissa, and they walked back to their table.

Theo looked up as they rejoined him. "So, I guess we're going?" he asked.

Melissa nodded enthusiastically.

Eliza was about to sit back down, when Theo intervened. "The bill's already been taken care of."

"Oh, thank you," Eliza responded. She grabbed her coat from the chair, and Melissa followed suit.

Within ten minutes, the three of them arrived at the bar. *Nelly's* was the same place where they'd met Theo the night before, and it was one of the most popular hangout spots in Birkbridge, especially on the weekends. Many of the locals, including Andrew, also frequented the *Beer Cave*, which was a more laid back and patriotic style bar. The cave theme referenced the famous Indiana caves, which were known primarily for being featured in the story of Huckleberry Finn. Eliza had sometimes accompanied Andrew during his bi-weekly hangouts with his friends. Sometimes they went on their own, but most of the time Eliza would find herself perched on a stool, watching Andrew playing pool with his friends. For this reason, she much preferred going to *Nelly's* with her friends. Granted, it was more crowded, but at least she didn't have to watch or play pool. Plus, the beer at *Nelly's* was much better suited to her taste.

As soon as they walked into *Nelly's*, Theo excused himself and disappeared to the bar. Meanwhile, Melissa and Eliza joined forces to try and hunt down an empty table. After circling the venue twice, they finally spotted a group leaving and took the vacant space.

Within a few minutes, Melissa spotted Theo approaching the table. As he got closer, it became apparent that he was walking over with another man. They approached the table, and they each set down two drinks.

"Let me introduce you," said Theo. "This is Hayden, my brother."

Chapter Five

Eliza and Melissa exchanged looks, unable to hide their surprise. Theo hadn't mentioned a brother, let alone told them that they would be meeting him at *Nelly's*.

Hayden stretched out his arm to Melissa. "It's nice to meet you. My brother's told me all about you."

"Oh, thank you," Melissa replied bashfully. She seemed taken aback by the fact that Theo had told his brother 'all about her', despite the fact that they'd only known each other for a few days. "I'm Melissa," she added hurriedly.

Hayden turned slowly to Eliza, allowing his eyes to graze her body lightly before finally making eye contact. He stretched out his hand.

"Hi, there," he said, his voice perking up. He turned to face his brother while still holding Eliza's hand, mid-handshake. "You didn't tell me that Melissa's friend was such a knockout."

Eliza laughed politely, at a loss about how to respond, and continued shaking his hand. Hayden's eyes met hers again, and Eliza had to fight the urge to look away. His look was so intense, and she wasn't sure whether she was comfortable with his presence. Had she just been tricked into a double date? Had Theo told his brother that she was free and willing? As these thoughts crowded her mind, Eliza replayed Hayden's opening line in her head. Somehow, it was a line that would've sounded cheesy coming from anyone else, but in Hayden's slow, caramel-laced voice, it had sounded incredibly sexy.

"My name's Eliza. It's nice to meet you, too," she said briskly.

The men sat down and raised their glasses. "Thanks for the drinks," Melissa said, smiling up at Theo. The two were getting cozier by the minute, and Theo had his arm around her. It struck Eliza as strange that, after only a few nights of knowing one another, they were already beginning to look and act like an item.

Eliza didn't want to risk sending Hayden the wrong signals, but she couldn't help but glance at him from the corner of her eye. She realized that her whole body had stiffened up, and she was holding her glass in front of herself defensively. "Yes, thanks so much for the drink, Theo, and also for the lovely dinner earlier. I don't want to be rude, but I really can't stay long. I promised Melissa I'd come along for a drink, but I should really get home soon. I promised my boyfriend I'd be home relatively early," she explained, trying desperately to sound matter-of-fact and light-hearted.

"That's a shame," said Hayden, throwing Eliza a quick glance. There was something so powerful in his gaze that Eliza's heart nearly skipped a beat.

"I know, I told her that she should stay longer, but she refuses to listen," Melissa chimed in.

"No, I meant that it's a shame she has a boyfriend," Hayden responded, ever so casually. He turned back to Eliza and locked eyes with her, refusing to retract his gaze.

Eliza was appalled by Hayden's audacity to speak so frankly to her, but she couldn't help but feel impressed by his unapologetic attitude. He was definitely the kind of man who took what he wanted and didn't look back.

Sensing the sexual tension, Melissa decided to cut in. "So, Hayden, what brings you to Birkbridge? Are you here to stay?"

"Yes, I am," he said, his voice remaining steady and slow. He didn't take his eyes off Eliza.

"I see," Melissa replied, the pitch of her voice rising. She was beginning to feel awkward since, after all, she had been the one to lure her friend into this unplanned double date. However, as any good friend, she was desperate to save the moment, so she continued talking. "So do you already have a job lined up?"

Slowly, Hayden turned back to Melissa and Theo, but his eyes remained glued to Eliza's for as long as possible before he inevitably looked away. It was as if his insides were made of caramel; his voice and his gaze had stickiness to them, an ability to linger. Even when he finished speaking, the sweetness of his voice still remained for a while longer, just like the taste of a delicious candy.

"I assumed that my brother had informed you about what it is we're doing here," he said mysteriously.

Melissa flashed Eliza a look of confusion, once more relying on the powers of friendship to send her friend telepathic messages. Whether or not Eliza was able to read her thoughts, it was clear that they were thinking along the same lines. *What were the brothers doing here? Were they spies, hired assassins? But why would assassins come to Birkbridge, Indiana?*

Before they could get too carried away in fantasyland, Eliza decided to speak up, forcing her voice to sound as casual as possible. She cleared her throat. "I'm not sure if Theo's mentioned it, but maybe you could inform us?"

Hayden flashed her a wide, cheeky smile. Even though he wasn't as classically handsome as his brother, there was something about the way that he held himself that made him a whole lot sexier.

"Well, to answer Melissa's question, my brother and I do have jobs here. We actually moved here to work in the coal mines," Theo responded. "We used to mine gold, but most of the active reserves have dried up. So we decided to return to coal mining, which has been a family legacy for many generations. Well… that and gold mining," he added, flashing Eliza a smile.

"Interesting, it's funny how common these family legacies are in the Midwest. My boyfriend's family also—"

"We're not from the Midwest," Hayden corrected her. She looked at him crossly, secretly suspecting that he cut her off on purpose just as she brought up her boyfriend.

"So where are you from?" Melissa inquired.

"Actually, nowhere," laughed Theo. "We're a family of drifters."

Melissa's eyes sparkled and she snuggled up closer to him. *Of course she'd be attracted to a drifter. It's always been her dream to leave this town, and now she's met someone who can help her to make that happen.*

"Theo's told me that you've lived in quite a lot of places, but I didn't realize that you moved around so often," Melissa said, addressing Hayden.

"Yes, well, it's not exactly something that we brag about," Hayden explained. "A lot of the towns that we come to are quite small, similar to this one, and from experience we've learned that people in towns like this aren't so... how would you call it... *open* to people with alternative lifestyles."

Melissa nodded knowingly, but Eliza didn't respond. She couldn't help but read between the lines, and she felt as if there was something more to these brothers' lives than they had chosen 'not to brag about'.

Perhaps it was due to her small-town upbringing, but Eliza wasn't too accustomed to secrets or surprises. Even though there were some oddballs living amongst the Birkbridge residents, at least she could make peace with the fact that virtually everybody knew everybody, either personally or through somebody else. For the first time in years, she was sitting next to somebody who she couldn't run a word-of-mouth background check on. It struck her that the brothers could tell them whatever they wanted, and she wouldn't have a clue whether they were just making all of it up. She would just have to go with her gut on this one.

It wasn't until then did Eliza realize she'd been noticing quite a few new faces walking around town over the past few weeks. She had heard people mention that there was an influx of new residents and workers that were the result of a hiring spree brought forth by the mines and the factory. Birkbridge hadn't seen a population increase like this for quite some time. Maybe she should suggest to Jim that they do a story about it? Anything would be better than covering livestock at this point. Eliza snapped herself back to the conversation. She was after all, off the clock and didn't want to seem rude to Melissa and her new beau.

They continued chatting for a while, and the tension between Eliza and Hayden eased a little. Perhaps the alcohol helped, or maybe Eliza just got accustomed to the intensity of his eyes. She was no longer trying to avoid his gaze, but she made sure to break eye contact every once in a while and chat to Melissa and Theo for a change. Soon enough, the brothers began telling stories and got caught in a competition of one-upping each other. They told stories of the road, stories about the gold rushes, and stories about their parents. They explained that their parents had died a long time ago, during an accident at a gold reserve. The reserve was in the mountains and an avalanche struck, which buried their parents under a pile of heavy rocks.

"I'm so sorry to hear that," Melissa said, gently stroking Theo's arm.

"You don't feel like you're in danger when you continue to work in the mines, despite what happened to your parents?" Eliza asked looking from one brother to the other.

Hayden's expression changed into a sad smile. "Well, what can we do? Things happen to people all the time, and every person finds themselves in potentially risky situations. The chances of dying in an avalanche are a lot lower than dying in a car accident. I think that it's certainly made us more careful, but it's also taught us to stick together. Mother and Father were together at the end, and that's all that anybody could wish for; to be surrounded by people, or a person, who you love before you die."

Eliza nodded.

"Do you have any other family?" Melissa asked.

"Yes, of course. But they don't like to settle down either, so in order to meet up, we have to mutually agree on a pre-determined location every single year."

"What's the location this year?" Melissa asked.

"That's a secret," Theo told her with mock-suspense. He bit her nose lightly and she giggled.

Eliza finally managed to excuse herself, and the others let her go. Hayden kissed her hand before she left, a gentlemanly action that seemed more suited for his brother. However, when Hayden did it, there was something about his manner that suggested he was doing this with self-irony. There was a hint of playfulness in his mannerisms that Eliza felt herself relating to. She was also quite big on sarcasm and irony, particularly when she was tired, anxious or drunk. She figured that she'd picked up this trait from her father, and had integrated it into her TV persona just enough to make herself funny while retaining her integrity.

The problem with Andrew was that he was such an all-or-nothing kind of guy that he didn't understand the gray areas. He could be very playful, but he was never subtle, which is one of the reasons that he didn't know how to flirt. When Andrew had asked Eliza out, there was no beating around the bush. Will you go for a coffee with me; will you come out on a dinner date with me; do you want to move in together? Even though Andrew's no-bullshit attitude had been what Eliza liked about him in the first place, she admitted to herself that it was all a little bit predictable. She didn't like playing games, but she wouldn't mind introducing some elements of surprise into her life. But Andrew was a man of routine. He thrived on birthdays and anniversaries, one-upping himself every single time. It was all incredibly romantic, but even romance had a funny way of seeming empty when it was repeated too many times.

As Eliza exited the bar, she couldn't help but feel like she was being watched. It was as if she was wearing a bulls-eye on her forehead, and every other woman in *Nelly's* was aiming a piercing glare directly at her. They tried to be subtle about it, but as their eyes darted between her and Hayden, she couldn't help but assume what they were all thinking. *What makes her so special? Why was she on a date with that sexy stranger, and why on earth is she leaving? Who does she think she is?*

It took every ounce of willpower in Eliza's body to stop herself from turning around and yelling, "I have a boyfriend!" to the entire bar. She wished that Andrew hadn't left so early. People were generally nicer to her when he was around.

The next morning was slow and lazy. Andrew didn't appear annoyed or inquisitive about Eliza's late departure from the bar, and although she was relieved that he didn't question her, she couldn't help but wish that he was a little more jealous. Of course, she was glad that he was not the jealous type, and she respected the fact that his complete faith in her was symptomatic of his own trustworthiness. According to his logic, he would never cheat on her, so why would she cheat on him?

Nevertheless, sometimes Eliza felt as if he just didn't think that another man would be attracted to her.

Of course, this was just her insecurity speaking, but a feeling was a feeling and it couldn't be shaken off just like that. She was only human, after all.

Despite the jumble of thoughts that were running through her mind, Eliza had a genuinely pleasant morning with Andrew. What was it about him that made her feel so comfortable and at ease around him? He was literally the opposite of the coal brothers, since the two of them were probably the most intimidating human beings who she'd ever come across. Hayden in particular.

For a moment, Eliza pondered whether she should tell Andrew about Hayden's presence the night before. Something weighed down on her that felt a bit like guilt and she wanted to rid herself of that feeling. She and Andrew never had secrets from one another; they usually told each other every little stupid thing. However, she told herself that there was no reason to feel guilty. *He didn't actually ask me if we met anyone else that night, and if he asks me, I'll tell him.* This made her feel a little bit better.

During brunch, a little Saturday tradition that the two of them had, dating back from their days at Andrew's apartment, Andrew informed her that he'd spoken to his friend, Tom, earlier that morning. Tom was one of Andrew's closest friends and also happened to be Brienne's husband. It was not uncommon in Birkbridge that everyone was connected in more than one way, either through friendships or familial relations. Eliza had actually met Brienne for the first time during one of the pool-table gatherings at the *Beer*

Cave. She'd been perched on the barstool, half-watching the game while partially zoning out and staring into space. Pool really had the effect of boring her half to death. All of a sudden, she had realized that somebody was trying to get her attention. It was Brienne. She was holding a pitcher of some kind of toxic-looking concoction, and she was holding it up under Eliza's nose.

"That smells strong," Eliza remarked.

"Well, you looked a bit spaced out and you weren't answering when I tried to talk to you, so I figured that this was my best shot at getting through to you."

"It definitely worked. That stuff smells nasty."

"Yeah. You want some?"

"Sure, why not."

Three months later, Eliza and Andrew found themselves at Tom and Brienne's wedding. Even Melissa was there because, as it turned out, Brienne and Melissa were actually friends from work, which was another one of those small-town coincidences.

As he munched down his eggs, Andrew told Eliza that Tom had recommended a few people who could help them with their painting and construction. Tom and Brienne had recently refurbished their own house, a necessity that had arisen after the birth of their third child. Tom said that the painter could come in at two o'clock that very same day, since he was a weekend contractor. During the week, he apparently worked at the concessions in their local movie theatre, but aside from his arrested development, Tom vouched that he was a reliable worker.

After brunch, Andrew went to the supply store and Eliza took a long, luxurious shower. Saturdays were her favorite days of the week because she was able to relax without feeling antsy. During the weekdays, she always felt as if she were slacking off when she wasn't busy. It was as if every moment wasted was a moment that she would eventually have to make up for. However, weekends seemed to be impervious to karmic powers, and she didn't feel like there were any dire consequences for taking it easy on a Saturday.

After her shower, Eliza got dressed and went back downstairs, just in time to open the door for the painter.

"Hi, come on in," she said, ushering him in.

The painter was a tall, stalky man with a bony face and a scraggly, unkempt beard. His hair was tied behind his head in a ponytail. As he walked through the door, Eliza caught him looking at her funny. She smiled awkwardly and tried to strike up a conversation by mentioning that Tom had recommended him. He politely nodded, but was still giving her a strange look. Now that she was looking at his face properly, Eliza realized that he looked familiar. *Everyone in Birkbridge looks familiar.*

Just as she thought that, the painter scratched his head awkwardly, his facial expression changing from anxious to apologetic.

"I uh…" he began, pausing to search for words. "I'm not sure if you'd remember me, but we went to school together when we were kids."

And like a brick smashing through a cardboard box, it suddenly dawned on her. This man was the grown-up version of the kid who had made her life a living hell in school. His name was Freddie Dormund.

Chapter Six

Freddie was one of those people who were easily underestimated in their potential for evil. From the outside, he appeared to be a pretty normal boy; most of the other kids didn't particularly like him or dislike him. Eliza and Freddie often sat together in classes, at first merely because they had nobody else to sit with.

When school began, Freddie had been a bit of a loner like Eliza, but unlike her, he was never content with being a fly on the wall. He was always trying to crack jokes and entertain the masses, but he was consistently shut down, told to be quiet, urged to sit still. Eventually, Freddie had been put on ADD medication, and to this day, Eliza was unsure whether the medication actually made him crazy, or it had just awakened something inside him that was dormant. Perhaps the drugs eased his social anxiety, and his newfound ability to interact with his peers was what drove him to become a sociopathic megalomaniac.

Whatever the causes, in their junior year of high school, it had begun to seem as if Freddie was put on this earth to make Eliza's life a living hell. But oddly enough, toward the end of the first year, they had actually begun to find more things in common than their mutual friendlessness.

Eliza hadn't kept in contact with Freddie much during the summer but they'd exchanged the odd text, mostly just inside jokes, and when Eliza came back to school the next semester, she sat next to Freddie in math class as usual. They chatted and caught up a little and everything seemed pretty normal. During lunch, Eliza noticed Freddie going off with some of the other kids from her grade. She was surprised but realized he must've made some friends during the summer. Eliza couldn't blame him, since she had essentially abandoned him in Birkbridge all season. After a while, Freddie grew more distant, but Eliza didn't want to impose herself on him. She figured that she was just destined to be a loner and retreated back into her isolated existence.

She didn't know exactly what happened, but every time she walked by him and his new group of friends and said hi to Freddie they would poke at him and he would turn red. She found out later through the grape vine that they accused Freddie of dating Eliza, and teased him endlessly about it.

After this incident, something snapped inside of Freddie. Eliza still wasn't sure whether it was his medication or whether he just couldn't handle the social pressure of being the object of ridicule amongst his new group of friends, but Freddie had suddenly made it his mission to prove that he had no feelings of affection toward Eliza and she made sure to stay out of his way. Nevertheless, it was impossible to avoid her classmate altogether. Freddie carried on bullying Eliza purely for entertainment. His daring comments and heartless jabs gained him a new level of respect from his friends, and he was beginning to feel truly accepted.

Thunderthighs was the name that Freddie had tossed at Eliza during junior year - nothing else had ended up sticking as prominently as this one. He'd come up with this particular gem during PE class, to which Eliza started wearing shorts. She usually wore regular sports pants, but they were having their spring classes outside and to her dismay, she noticed an entire group of her classmates, with Freddie at the front, staring at her from the other side of the football field. As always, Freddie operated covertly, cleverly avoiding the watchful gaze of the teachers.

Eliza didn't want to know what they were saying, but her curiosity and embarrassment got the best of her. During the final lap of the one-mile run, Eliza made sure to run by Freddie's friends. As she ran past them, she could faintly make out the awful words. "Look at *Thunderthighs* go! Take cover, there's a storm coming!" Afterward, she wished with all her heart that she hadn't been listening.

Chapter Seven

By the time Andrew came back, Eliza had managed to regain her cool. After Freddie's arrival, she went through several stages of panic. The first stage was detachment and coldness; she acted as if her selective memory had erased the awful details of her past.

"Oh yes, Freddie, of course, I remember you. We sat together in Math," she had said robotically.

Freddie looked at her oddly, but then his face softened as he realized that he might be 'off the hook'. *That stupid asshole thinks that I forgot all about it.* At this point, she was already entering the following stage of panic, which was epitomized by a searing rage. Rage at him, rage at herself; she even felt angry toward Andrew just for not being there at that very moment. She began to feel angry and alone in the world. Tears welled up inside her eyes, but she had to control them.

"Please, help yourself to any snacks in the kitchen, and you can get started whenever you need. My boyfriend's gone out to get some additional paint, but we have a few cans ready for you outside, so maybe you can get started with those."

"Sure, thank you," Freddie replied. He seemed not only a little *slow*, but also somehow braindead. She realized that the rumors must've been true, even though she had ignored them at the time, since she hadn't wanted to think about Freddie in any context, even a negative one. During the last year of high school, Freddie had barely passed. In fact, it was a miracle that he had graduated at all. At the time, it had become known that Freddie's ADD medication had driven him into some dark state of mind, which reflected badly on his behavior and grades. However, there were also the rumors; some kids were saying that Freddie had been taken off his medication, but because he had become addicted to it, he had sought after other drugs in replacement. Even though these rumors seemed believable right now, the kids at high school had found it difficult to believe this, since nobody else in their year had ever experimented with hard drugs, and therefore did not really understand how Freddie could've scored them. Now that Eliza evaluated Freddie's beat-down appearance, using the context of possible drug abuse, the rumors actually started making sense. She realized that they were most likely completely true.

This realization brought the third stage of panic, which was a manic embodiment of malicious joy. As a firm believer in the vindictive powers of karma, Eliza realized that at last, justice had been served! She excused herself, leaving the sad, dried-up drug addict to attend to her household chores. She felt good about this, almost too good. By the time Eliza walked into her room, she was bouncing up and down.

She realized that she really wanted a drink. She reached for her bedside cabinet, where she kept a not-so-secret little bottle of whisky stashed. This was mostly meant for work-related fiascos or late-night-girl-drama phone calls from her friends, mostly Melissa.

At this particular moment, the tiny bottle seemed to have Eliza's name written all over it.

She twisted the lid off rabidly and chugged the contents. At this moment, she started to enter the fourth panic stage: a flood of raw emotion. All the other stages mixed into one big ball of rage, numbness, sadness and happiness. She was angry that the person who had made her life miserable had the audacity to walk into her home and think that she had forgotten what he'd done to her. She was sad that she allowed him to make her feel this way, despite the fact that she was living such a happy and fulfilled life. She was happy that Andrew would be home any minute, and that they would kick this asshole out together, and that she could continue living her life while Freddie returned to his miserable teen-boy job at the movie theatre.

Andrew arrived twelve minutes and twenty tissues later, by which point the booze had hit Eliza and she was back to stage one; numbness. She was lying on the bed, staring up at the wall, where a framed photograph of her and Andrew hung. They were smiling, and Eliza tried to smile back at them, her mouth forming into a crooked half-smile but her eyes remaining cold.

"Hey there, sleepyhead," he said with a soft laugh, kissing her on the forehead.

"Ummh…" she groaned, not wanting to speak yet.

"You ok? I saw the guy outside, he seems nice. A little weird though, if you know what I mean. I thought ponytails like that were reserved for rednecks in Hollywood films."

"Yeah, he's an oddball. I used to go to school with him," Eliza said monotonously.

"Really? I didn't know that."

"Well neither did I, until he walked through our front door."

"Are you sure you're ok? He didn't say anything that bothered you, did he? Because if he did, I can definitely get rid of him, give him like half a day's pay."

"No, he didn't say anything. We used to get along in school for a while but then we kind of just stopped being friends. I guess it was just weird to see him, that's all."

Andrew perched on the edge of the bed and observed Eliza carefully. "Hmm… he sounds like a jerk. Anyone who would give up your friendship must be a total lunatic."

Eliza smiled weakly.

"I'll get rid of him," Andrew said.

"It's ok, he didn't say anything to me. We can let him finish up," Eliza said defensively. She wasn't sure why she was suddenly acting so defensive. Freddie was clearly a source of a lot of psychological pain for her, but she didn't seem capable of revealing that side of herself to Andrew. She had always been honest with him, but perhaps she just wasn't ready to expose her deep-seated adolescent insecurities to her boyfriend. Maybe, deep down, she was afraid that if she spoke about the girl she used to be, Andrew might start to see her for that very girl; shy, lonely, unliked, unattractive. She had fought long and hard to reverse those traits and had succeeded in doing so. Eliza wasn't ready to give up all that hard work, so she put on a brave face.

"We can tell him that we only needed him today, and maybe make up some excuse about my distant cousin who's coming over to help us tomorrow. We can say he's doing it for free or something," she offered.

"Whatever you say," Andrew agreed, smiling at her sudden ability to make up a slightly farfetched yet practically impenetrable alibi for firing their newly hired painter.

He stood up, looking around for a second, then shrugged his shoulders and plopped onto the bed. "You might be onto something with the going-back-to-bed thing. Maybe we can make this our Saturday tradition, too?"

Eliza laughed and swung her right leg over her boyfriend, pulling him close. They stayed in bed until the sun went down.

In the evening, Andrew walked downstairs to pay Freddie and explain to him that his services would no longer be needed, but it seemed that he had missed him by half an hour. He found a text message on his phone from Freddie, who explained that he was heading home and that he would be back tomorrow. Even though Andrew didn't normally do this, he ended up having to fire Freddie via text message.

<<◇>>

As usual, Brienne called up on Sunday. Everyone seemed to have a favorite day of the week, and Brienne was a big fan of the Sabbath day. She was a proud mother and her kids meant the world to her, but just like any job came with a holiday, motherhood certainly required a little break once in a while. Sunday was Tom's day with the kids, and therefore Brienne's official day off. As a senior executive at Millstone Firearms, Tom was a very busy man, who rarely got to see his kids during his eleven-hour workdays. But on Sunday, he had all the time in the world. He would plan fun trips, which usually involved the zoo, but sometimes also go-carting, bowling or laser tag. Of course, Brienne had come along sometimes, but ever since her youngest child was born, she had been too exhausted to join in with Sunday fun times. Instead, she preferred to take it easy and call up her girlfriends.

Usually, Brienne was up early, and she would call Eliza around ten. They would meet for coffee either at Eliza's place or at some café. Following Melissa's suggestion, they agreed to venture out into Wakefield, a nearby town. Melissa usually didn't come along on their Sunday meetups because she was either too hungover or visiting her mother. Ever since she met Theo, three days ago, Melissa had given up partying, and this particular Sunday she had dialed Eliza before the latter had even gotten out of bed. Apparently, Melissa wanted to discuss something pretty serious with the other two. *They better not be getting married.*

Eliza, Melissa and Brienne met up in the town and walked around for a little while until they found a cozy coffee shop to hang out in. It was a cold but sunny day, and it felt nice to walk around unfamiliar territory. Eliza used to see new and exciting places for work, but as of late these instances had become fewer and fewer.

When they got their table, Melissa was finally ready to talk to them about her big dilemma.

"So, as you probably already know, Theo and I have been seeing a lot of each other lately," she began.

Brienne nodded eagerly. By the look of Brienne's face, Eliza could tell that she wasn't the only one who'd suspected that Melissa's news would have something to do with a proposal. But unlike Brienne, this thought didn't really excite Eliza, since she didn't understand how it was possible to marry someone after knowing them for only four days. After all, Eliza and Andrew weren't married and they'd had a relationship lasting over six years.

Melissa raised her eyebrow at Brienne's over-amplified eagerness. "As I was saying…" she continued, "I know that I just met him, and it's a little early, but I've decided that I want to…"

Without realizing it, Eliza uttered a high-pitched yelp.

Melissa cocked her head. "What is *up* with the two of you? What I was going to say was, I wanted to introduce Theo to my mother."

"Oh, of course." Eliza nodded.

"What did you think I meant?" Melissa inquired, head still cocked to one side.

"Nothing," the other two muttered.

After pausing to think for a moment, the cogs began to turn in Brienne's head. She had a knack for connecting the dots and figuring out situations before they were laid out to her explicitly. "So your dilemma is that you're unsure whether your mother might flip out when she realizes that, not only are you getting serious with a man that you *just* met, but you're also dating one of the only men in this town who hasn't lived here for a bajillion years."

Brienne paused for air and continued talking. "*But*, you think that the positives might outweigh the negatives, and that if your mother meets this man and sees how happy you are with him, she might begin to trust your judgment and, most importantly, she'll finally realize that you're a grown woman and not just her poor little daughter who's been forced into premature adulthood due to the burden of looking after your sick mother."

"That's actually pretty accurate," Melissa admitted.

Brienne held up her finger to signify that she wasn't done yet. "There's more to it than that. I can tell that this isn't just about you. I think that you believe that this information might help your mother somehow in her recovery. But how…" Brienne paused to think for a second.

Melissa opened her mouth to answer the question, but Brienne put up her finger again.

"Unless... unless you believe that if your mother sees that you're all grown up, she might be willing to move back into the house. Perhaps if she realizes that she's no longer a burden, she might not feel so ashamed to live with you anymore."

Melissa and Eliza looked at Brienne, blinking stupidly. The same thought was running through both of their minds; *how does she do it?*

"That and, there's one more thing," Melissa said, the corner of her mouth bending into a mysterious sideways smile. She seemed proud of the fact that Brienne hadn't been able to unearth *all* of her secret schemes within the span of two minutes. "I've also asked Theo to move in with me, or 'us' if my mother agrees to move back in."

Eliza couldn't help smiling despite the prickling concern that this might have all been a bit too rushed. She had moved in with Andrew after less than a year of dating, but they had already become accustomed to being around one another almost every day, as well as most nights. Even though Theo seemed like the full package from the outside, how could Melissa tell whether he would be good to live with or not? He may be an exceptionally attractive person, but he was still a new person in her life, and everyone had at least some sort of irritating trait that revealed itself when you lived with them.

Melissa could sense the concern emanating from Eliza. "I know what you're thinking, but it's not as rushed as it sounds. He won't be moving in just yet, since he and his brother have housing from the mining authorities anyhow. However, it can be really depressing to live in the mines if you have no other home to return to on the weekends. So that's all that our arrangement concerns for the time being… *weekends*. Even then, Theo said that he and his brother sometimes have other things to attend to, so even the weekends aren't set in stone. What I'm trying to say is, we're going to be testing the waters. We'll get to see whether we like living together, and maybe someday he'll move in with me. And if he does, there will be two of us around to help mother when she needs it. Bless her, she still looks youthful as ever, but she's starting to get to an older age. Even if she agrees to leave the mental ward and announces herself 'cured', she'll still probably need some help with basic care. And I'm the only one she's got."

Eliza nodded in agreement. She understood that Melissa meant well, and that she kept her mother in mind with every decision she ever made. Objectively, this seemed like a really good plan, and Eliza admitted to herself that Theo seemed like a really decent guy. However, as she listened to Melissa talk to Brienne about Theo, she couldn't help but remember the gut feeling that she'd had around the brothers. She remembered the way that Theo had brushed off

Melissa's question when she'd asked him where they would have their next family gathering. "That's a secret," he'd said, playfully. Eliza wondered how many times Theo would get away with answering questions in that way. How many secrets did their family have? And as for his brother Hayden…

Eliza's thought was interrupted by the ringing of a phone. Instinctively, all three women reached for their pockets. It was Melissa's phone, and judging by the smile on her face, it was Theo.

Melissa got up and left for a little while to chat on the phone. Immediately, Brienne spun around to face Eliza. "So, you've met this man twice then? What do you think?"

"I think he's really nice. You saw him as well, didn't you? That first time at the bar."

"Yeah, but all I saw was the back of his head. How was the rest of him?"

"Bri, he's almost too good looking. Like a male model *after* photoshop."

"Sounds… a bit too cyborgy for my tastes but, nevertheless, dreamy."

"He's one dreamy cyborg," Eliza agreed. She could tell that Brienne was trying to play mind games to unearth Eliza's true thoughts about Theo, but she wasn't about to give them up so easily.

Brienne wasn't one to give up easily, so she pushed on. "Do you think he's monogamous? I mean, there's

no chance that he has anyone on the side, right?
Because that would be a primary concern that we
should probably check out before we let him move in
with her."

Eliza laughed. "First of all, we can't stop them from
moving in together. And to answer your question, I
obviously don't know much about the guy, but he
seems really into Melissa. Almost *too* into her."

"What do you mean, *too* into her?" Brienne seemed
to perk up again, her eyes darting around as if she were
trying to decipher something.

"No, nothing. I think that he really likes her, that's
all."

"Can you give me any more details?"

Eliza laughed again. Brienne wasn't letting this go,
so she figured she would give her *something*. "Just the
way he looks at her is really intense, you know? The
first night when we met him, Melissa was a little
wasted. And when she was in that state, I think he let
his guard down a little, and I caught him just full-on
staring at her. It weirded me out a little, but probably
only because he was a stranger at the time. I think I've
done too many newscasts about attempted rapes and
jailed perverts, so I guess I read into his look a little too
much and just profiled it as 'predatory'. But it's really
just desire, you know, lust or whatever."

"Riiight," Brienne said, still evidently lost in
thought. Eliza knew that Brienne would overanalyze the
living daylights out of this, but she was glad that she'd

distracted her friend for long enough. After all, Eliza had only shared a small fraction of her concerns. She made a promise to herself that she wouldn't tell Bri about her hunch that Theo and Hayden were hiding something.

Brienne looked like she was about to ask another Theo-related question, when Melissa came back. *Saved by the Mel*, Eliza thought. Melissa was still holding the phone to her ear, but after 'uhum'-ing a few times, she handed the phone over to Eliza.

Eliza hesitated. "Why does he want to speak to me?" she half-whispered, half-mouthed.

"It's Hayden," Melissa mouthed back, exaggeratedly.

Eliza sighed and snatched the phone from Melissa's mouth. She was prepared to cut this conversation short. *Who does he think he is, calling me when he knows that I have a boyfriend?* Besides, Brienne was sitting right next to her, and she was married to Andrew's best friend from work. Eliza figured that it would look suspicious if she left the table for the conversation, so she stayed put.

"Hi," she said neutrally.

There was a shuffling sound on the other end. Then, she heard that caramel-laced voice. "Hi, Eliza, I was hoping I could talk to you for a second. Is this an ok time?"

"I'm not sure. I'm with my friends, as you probably know since you spoke to Melissa just now."

"Right, of course, sorry to disturb you," Hayden said, his voice remaining steady and light. "I was just hoping to chat with you, but I don't have your number. I know it would've been sleazy if I just asked Melissa to give it to me, so I thought I'd ask you myself."

Eliza made an effort to appear unfazed, since she could feel Brienne and Melissa looking at her contemplatively. "Sure, but why do you need it?"

Hayden chuckled on the other end. "Your friends are sitting right there, aren't they?"

"That would be correct."

"In that case, I won't embarrass you any longer. I just wanted to call because, like I said, I didn't want to be a sleaze ball. I can ask Theo to get your number for me from Melissa. Just say 'yes' if you're ok with it and 'no' if you're not, and I won't bother you anymore."

Chapter Eight

"Yes," Eliza responded instantly, as if a supernatural force had taken her body hostage for that instant. She was shocked at her own words but knew that it was too late to take it back.

"Great," Hayden responded, audibly surprised but excited. "I'll call you tomorrow then. Have fun with your friends."

"Ok, you have a good day, too," Eliza replied robotically. She hung up the phone and passed it to Melissa.

Melissa was staring at her quizzically. "And?" she inquired.

"Nothing really," Eliza replied, shrugging her shoulders nonchalantly.

"What did he want to speak to you about?"

"Not really sure. I mean he asked me if this was a good time to talk, and I said I was with friends, so he said he'd call me back."

"Right." Melissa wasn't looking convinced. "Well, let me know what he tells you later. If it's something to do with Theo, you absolutely have to tell me."

Eliza smiled, relieved that Melissa was too preoccupied with Theo to entertain the notion of Hayden's insistent flirtations with Eliza.

<<◇>>

The following day was an office day for Eliza. This meant that the reporters, crew and network managers were going to be stuck in a tedious stream of meetings, during which they would also be viewing the footage from the previous week and deciding how to compile the pre-recorded shots to insert into the live news broadcasts.

If there was anything that Eliza enjoyed less than doing broadcasts about three-day fairs that revolved around growing the biggest, fattest farm animals, it was *watching* herself doing broadcasts about three-day fairs that revolved around growing the biggest, fattest farm animals. She knew that she would look ridiculous in her stupid windbreaker, which hadn't even done such a great job of protecting her from the incessant dribble of rain. Jim, of course, would love the bad weather aspect. However, Eliza didn't understand how he could've stooped as low as allowing three whole days for that garbage. If there was one consolation, it would be seeing Jim showing signs of disapproval. *This will show him what a bad idea it all was, and maybe it'll force him into acting like himself again. If all goes well, he'll say 'this is crap, let's do something awesome', and I'll finally get a good story.*

Contrary to her expectations, Jim breezed through the meetings in a suspiciously good mood. He was even acting a little manic, and his craziness reminded Eliza of a man in love. She hadn't seen Jim behave that way ever, probably due to the fact that he was gay and married to a woman. Nevertheless, Eliza suspected that he'd had affairs outside of his marriage, and even considered that he and Feline had some sort of special arrangement. After all, they seemed like great friends, and perhaps she became his beard for her own secret reasons. Maybe Feline was gay, too? Nobody really knew the truth, and since Jim was a perfect orchestrator of illusion, he had managed to keep his life incredibly discreet.

Jim approved the livestock fair footage and, to Eliza's dismay, decided that they should do 'more features like this' to 'please their Midwestern target audience'. And the more Jim kept insisting that the boring broadcasts were somehow a good thing, the more Eliza grew suspicious. She decided that she would have a little talk with her boss and confront him once and for all. Eliza had been with Jim from the beginning, and she had supported him through thick and thin. When she first came to work for him, she had just given up her Boston job offer, and it seemed like an odd move for her to start working for a minor news network. After two years of shooting guerilla-style broadcasts with Jim and his very limited crew, the ratings had finally shot up enough for Jim to receive real sponsorship. The only loose end he needed to tie up was the matter of his private life, and after his wedding to Feline, this was all settled. Three years later, their network ratings were in the stratosphere. They now had offices all throughout Indiana, and their stories were no longer purely Birkbridge-based. However, after all these years of hard work, it seemed as if Jim was returning to the small-scale stuff, under a guise of 'appealing to their target audience', aka farmers and suburban housewives.

Eliza, more than anyone, knew how much Jim hated being confronted. Having come from a big family, Jim's life had largely consisted of prying and confrontations. Ever since he was a child, he had been different from his male cousins and siblings. His father didn't seem to mind too much, but his mother and aunts seemed to have conspired to make Jim's life one large obstacle. 'Why don't you leave your sisters to play with their dolls and go outside, kick a ball around?' 'Don't you want to be like your older brothers?' 'Your father would be very proud of you if you joined the football team. You know that your father was one of the best players in his high school team?'

To make matters worse, Jim was the youngest child and therefore naturally a magnet for overbearing attention. The youngest child curse was unfortunately for life, and even when Jim had grown past his teen years, there was still a flurry of expectations for him to 'be like his brothers'. The comparisons never tired, and Jim had grown accustomed to zoning out the sound of nagging family members.

Even though she knew Jim wouldn't enjoy being scolded by her, Eliza knew that it was her duty to do it. Who else would ever confront him without the fear of being fired? Luckily, she was immune to this possibility, since as one of the core employees of the company, firing her would cost Jim a fortune. In fact, Eliza mused, being fired wouldn't be such a bad thing, considering how much money she would receive. *I could finally go on that culinary trip to Italy...* But this was all just fantasy; Eliza knew that she would never be able to give up journalism, unless it was for a life-changing cause. Her father had kept his job, in spite of the obvious dangers, until the very day that his wife announced her pregnancy.

Furthermore, Jim was Eliza's friend, and she knew that there was a chance that that stubborn man might actually listen to her. She grabbed her emergency bottle of wine from her desk drawer and headed to his office. Although it was strange to keep wine in a desk drawer, Eliza knew that this was the only drink that Jim actually liked, so she kept it around to deal with his relatively frequent outbursts. Speaking of which, his recent lack of outbursts was also a worrying factor. Maybe he really was losing his marbles?

"Eliza!" Jim exclaimed, a little too much enthusiasm lingering in his voice. "What are we celebrating?"

"Jim, you should know by now that this is crisis wine, it's not celebration wine."

"Ok… so does this mean that you're having a crisis?"

"No, you are," Eliza blurted out. The words had sounded a lot better in her head.

To her surprise, Jim wasn't bothered by her attitude. In fact, his expression was frustratingly calm. He smiled a little, feigning complete ignorance. "El, I'm not having a crisis."

"Well, something's definitely up with you. And if you can't be bothered to tell me, I'll figure it out myself."

"You would never guess," Jim said, his voice turning soft and dreamlike.

"What's that supposed to mean?" Eliza's eyes narrowed as she studied Jim's face. "You met someone, didn't you?"

"What on earth are you talking about, Eliza? I have a beautiful, loving wife," Jim said, his voice neutral enough to hide the deep-seated sarcasm.

"Ok, cut the shit," Eliza said, surprising herself once more with how forward she was being.

Jim's poker face dissipated and the corners of his mouth curled up into a smile. He began laughing.

Eliza just looked at him for a few moments, at which point she also caught the laughing bug. Before she knew it, they were both giggling and laughing.

Three quarters of crisis wine later, Jim began spilling the beans. He didn't want to go into specifics, but he met a devastatingly handsome man during the weekend. Jim said that the man was from out of town, and that they ran into one another at the supermarket, of all places. The man, Dylan, had been looking for a ready meal, and had asked Jim's opinion about what to get.

"I'm not sure which one will taste less like garbage, have you got any suggestions?" he'd inquired, flashing Jim a sexy smile. The sexy smile part was featured in Jim's recollection of this event, but Eliza couldn't be sure if this had been added onto the story later in order to spice it up.

"I'm afraid to say that they all taste like garbage," Jim had told him.

Apparently Dylan loved the joke, but had suddenly stopped laughing and looked at Jim quizzically. "Hey, do I know you from somewhere? I swear I've met you before."

"I don't think so, I would've definitely remembered meeting you," Jim said.

After scratching his head for a moment, Dylan had given up trying to figure out where he knew him from. Thereafter, Jim suggested that he may have seen him on TV, but that probably would've been a long time ago. He proceeded to tell him that he used to be a news anchor in Los Angeles during the 1990s. This made Dylan perk up considerably, and he excitedly proclaimed that he had watched Jim's broadcasts in LA, where he had lived with his family during his childhood and part of his adolescence.

"Let me guess," Eliza intervened, "he was what… five at the time?"

Jim didn't believe that her snarky comment warranted a response, so he just continued talking. Long story short, after chatting to Dylan for at least twenty minutes in the supermarket, Jim ended up offering to help cook dinner. "You can't be buying that microwavable garbage. It's much better to make a real meal."

For obvious reasons, they chose to go to Dylan's place rather than Jim's. Eliza was still too modest to ask Jim whether he and his wife had some sort of polygamous 'arrangement', but figured that she would ask him someday, if her curiosity got the better of her. Dylan lived in an apartment on the north side of town, near the coal mines. He told Jim that he was recruited to work in the mines during a recent staff deficit, and had only recently moved into Birkbridge and his new apartment.

Eliza realized that Hayden and Theo must also have responded to the same call to arms. It seemed that, as male unemployment soared in the country, there was still always work in the mines. Of course, due to obvious health risks and the stress of relocation, mine work was not suited for everybody. Generally, only young, single men would come to work in the mines, and even they would usually quit after a year or two. Eliza wondered how Theo and Hayden were able to stay healthy despite continuously working in dirty, dusty conditions. Gold mines, coal mines… perhaps their family had developed some kind of genetic immunity through the magic of Darwinian evolution. After all, they had said that the nomadic, gold-mining lifestyle had been in their bloodline for at least two centuries.

"So, what happened when you got to his apartment?" Eliza asked while pouring out the remainder of the wine bottle into Jim's glass. He smiled at her sleepily and Eliza was shocked that he was still spitting out information about his private life; this was so unlike Jim. *I should get him drunk more often.*

"Well, at first I cooked for him. It was a nightmare though because everything in that apartment was stiff and rusty, but you know me, I can always make do with what I've got."

Eliza nodded in agreement, thinking back on their crappy news studio days from five years ago. *We managed to make pretty great stuff.*

"So I managed to make a pretty good pasta dish," Jim continued, "and then time just slowed down, and it was almost like a movie. It just happened so naturally. I wasn't even sure if the man was gay or not; I can usually tell, but he was so damn *mysterious*, I really didn't know. I thought that I was going to have to make the move, but there I was, stirring the pasta sauce, when I felt his hands on my back, slowly moving down toward my…"

As the story heated up, Eliza put her glass of wine down with more oomph than she had realized, and the sound made Jim come back to his senses. "Oh, sorry, did I digress?"

"Just a little," Eliza admitted.

"Ok, well, to wrap up my story, it was the most amazing night I've ever had. *Ever.* Including my twenties at the LA broadcasting network. This just blew it all out of the water. Maybe because he was a complete stranger, or maybe because he was the hottest man in a 100-mile radius from this dump, but whatever the reason was, I still can't stop thinking about it."

"Are you seeing him again?"

"You can bet your bonus money on that, missy."

When Eliza sobered up and drove home, she realized that she hadn't even had a proper talk with Jim about the important work stuff that she'd really needed to confront him about. *I guess that ship has sailed... I'll just be reporting on donkey shit for the rest of my life.* She was very happy for Jim that he'd met a guy who turned his world upside down, but she couldn't help but reflect his happiness onto her own self-pity. Everyone seemed to be happy with this sudden gold-rush of hot coal-miners that had flooded their boring little town.

The sexy story that Jim had told her also began to resonate with a darker, repressed side of her inner psyche. Eliza had never questioned her sexual attraction for Andrew, since he had always been an objective 'hottie'. She had thought he was handsome, albeit slightly cocky, from the moment she met him. All her friends thought he was good looking and charming, and so did the girls who knew him in college. But when she tried to apply the chemistry and passion that were central to Jim's story to her sexual relationship with Andrew, Eliza began to see that something was missing. Ever since she'd started dating Andrew, she hadn't felt this numb. For the first time since high school, she was starting to feel a personality crisis coming on.

Her drive home was an emotional rollercoaster, and to make matters even more complicated, Eliza received a phone call. The number was anonymous, but she had a feeling that she knew who it was. *Should I pick up?*

Without giving herself time to think anymore, Eliza pressed the 'accept call' button on her car loudspeaker. "Hello, this is Eliza speaking," she said formally.

"Hi, Eliza, it's Hayden."

"Hayden, hi. What did you want to speak to me about the other day?"

"It was nothing in particular actually, but I just wanted a chance to talk to you alone. Listen, I know that you have a boyfriend and I respect that you were upfront about it, but I'd really like a chance to spend time with you, just as friends. I've hung out with my brother much too often since we got here, plus now he also has Melissa. I need a friend, and believe it or not, I wasn't only interested in talking with you because you're beautiful. I thought you were interesting, and I think that you're an upfront and honest person."

Eliza's concerns from earlier, her worries about Jim and Andrew evaporated for a moment. She hadn't realized that Hayden was lonely and looking for a friend, but his outpouring made her suddenly want to trust him. She realized that she needed a friend as well, since all her other friends were too intertwined in her life to trust with her doubts and worries.

"Ok," Eliza said firmly, "tell you what, I have a free afternoon tomorrow, so maybe we can meet to talk over coffee?"

"Sounds good to me," Hayden replied, his voice enunciating each syllable in a deliciously smooth way.

"Good, I'll text you the directions."

Eliza hung up the phone before he could respond, since she didn't want to get sucked into a deeper conversation at the moment. Her mind was still conflicted about her recent revelation regarding her sex life, and she was determined to try and right this wrong. As soon as she got home, she would seduce her boyfriend, they would have amazing sex, and she would hereby prove to herself that they had chemistry.

By the time that Eliza got up to the bedroom, Andrew was already in the shower. She lay down on the bed and waited for him to come out.

Five minutes later, Andrew emerged with a towel around his waist. His body was still glistening with drops of water, which slid down his body and dripped off his strong, manly legs. "Hey you, where've you been all this time?"

"I had to have a talk with my boss, and then I had to wait to sober up before I drove home."

"Oh no, Eliza, did he…"

"No, no, nothing like that!" Eliza assured him. "I was actually the one who called our little meeting."

Andrew looked surprised but impressed. "My girlfriend, the power player who makes her boss go to meetings," he teased.

"What did you talk about?"

"Ehm, well we ended up talking about some weird stuff, but initially I just wanted to confront him about all the boring broadcasts he's had us doing."

Andrew laughed dismissively. "Eliza, stop saying that those reports are so boring. You're insulting the intelligence of our town. Everyone loves your reports, and viewership has never been better. I watched your report today, the one about the fair, and I really liked it."

"It's not that *the people* don't like it. I'm just saying that we could do a lot better. Jim gained popularity by using the simple premise of looking beyond the ordinary. He knew that people needed a break from their daily routines, and he was willing to hunt for the stories that would provide them that. It's not *escapist* per se, but it's more about finding stories that are fresh and interesting. As a broadcasting company, it's our job to help people learn new facts about life through showing them extraordinary real-life situations. And the livestock fair, for me, stands for everything that we're against. It's predictable; it's annual; it's planned; it's boring… tedious."

Eliza took a breath, surprised at her sudden anger toward this topic. "Also," she continued, "I don't think that *I'm* the one who's insulting the intelligence of this town. It's Jim who's doing so, because he thinks that our 'target audience' will be so incredibly happy to accept repetitive, recycled stories as news!"

"Eliza… the thing about finding these phenomenal events, is that they're usually tragic. Things that just *happen* are usually shootings, car accidents… at best sexual harassment lawsuits. I know that you respect your father, but what made his work fed off tragedy. And I think that, although reporting these things is part of your work, it's also your job to report about the positive things that happen. People like to see their own reality reflected on a TV screen. Excitement can be found from within ordinary life, not just from outside of it."

Eliza sighed. Even though Andrew made a valid point, she had still been hoping that he would at least *understand* her point of view. It seemed as if he was not just defending the Birkbridge mentality, but he was *choosing* it over her. Eliza felt alone and misunderstood. Jim, Andrew, even Brienne and Melissa; people who she considered close to her did not seem to *understand* her. Maybe she was the one who had changed… maybe she was the unsympathetic member of her community. Eliza felt as if she was turning into her father, and she couldn't even control it.

Andrew and Eliza had one main rule in their household… never go to bed angry. The only other rule was 'don't leave your hair straightener on', which was insisted on by Andrew, following an almost disastrous incident. Eliza no longer straightened her hair anyway, since she learned to tame her long brown locks with a round brush and anti-frizz spray.

That night was no exception to the main rule, and the couple made sure to talk out their differences before hitting the hay. However, the long talk had also ruined Eliza's seduction plan from earlier. She almost wished that they'd gone to bed angry because this could've ignited some sparks of passion, which perhaps would've led to some amazing make-up-sex.

Unfortunately, the moment had passed, since after an hour of talking and making peace, Eliza was emotionally and physically exhausted. As she fell asleep in Andrew's arms, she couldn't help but think that their ground rule might be in need of re-evaluation.

On Tuesday, Eliza had yet another free morning. Ever since Jim had lost his media spark, the free mornings had become increasingly frequent. Most people would be happy to get some extra spare time, but Eliza wasn't most people. She had been such a workaholic for the past five years, that she rarely had a minute to herself other than on the weekends. And even her weekends were tightly packed and scheduled with trips and plans to see friends or family.

The thing that scared Eliza about being alone was the thought that inevitably penetrated her mind. Her relationship with Andrew seemed happy to her, but they had also been so busy for the past few years that they hardly spent any time alone. This thought brought panic to Eliza's mind; was her love with Andrew just a sham? Did they still have a spark? Had they *ever* had a spark?

As these worrying thoughts clouded her mind, Eliza realized that she had promised to meet Hayden for coffee in an hour. She quickly showered, dried her hair, and applied some eyeliner and mascara. Eliza was swift and precise when it came to makeup… a skill that she had perfected after being on-camera for five years. Eliza looked at herself in the mirror and couldn't help but admire the results. For a forty-five-minute routine, she was looking astoundingly good.

She was about to leave when she remembered that she'd left her phone in the bathroom, so she went to fetch it. At that moment, the doorbell rang. *Has Hayden showed up at my house?*

Eliza ran over to the door and swung it open. It wasn't Hayden… it was Freddie.

Chapter Nine

Damn it. Eliza had forgotten that Freddie was coming by to collect his paycheck that morning. *Right, no reason to panic. Don't let him see that he still gets to you. Just give him the check and send him on his way.*

"One second," Eliza said as she retreated into the house to pick up her checkbook. Freddie stood outside the door awkwardly, but she wasn't about to let him into her home again.

She emerged from the living room and handed him a piece of paper with a rather generous amount, which she scribbled on just to get rid of him sooner.

"I was supposed to be paid in cash," Freddie insisted in a low drawl. His words were partially slurred and his vacant look suggested that he was going through some sort of drug-induced hangover.

"I don't have any cash on me. I've written you a generous check for your five hours of work." Eliza's tone was taking on hints of frustration, but she maintained calm and control.

"I don't take checks."

"Then I'll talk to my boyfriend, and we'll see what we can do. Come back tomorrow."

"I wanna speak to him now," Freddie said aggressively. Before Eliza knew it, he pushed past her and marched into the living room.

"Andrew's not here at the moment," she told him loudly and firmly. She was on the verge of panic, but she didn't want to let it show. *Freddie feeds off fear, don't let him catch you cowering.*

"I think you should leave, and we will contact you about the money," she told him sternly.

"And *I* think that I'll just wait here until that boyfriend of yours comes home with my money!" Freddie yelled.

Eliza couldn't take this anymore. Her head was splitting with a roaring headache, and her nerves were on the verge of convulsing into a fit of panic. "Get out of my house, Freddie!" she shouted at the top of her lungs. Her eyes were wild with rage as she stared up at his thick, sullen face. *How dare he stand here and demand money from me?*

Freddie stared back at her with a look that was barely human. His eyes filled up with a rabid look of pure, sadistic loathing.

"You think you're so much better than everyone, don't you?" Freddie snarled.

Eliza stood dead in her tracks. She refused to let her gaze drop. Freddie was just like a vicious dog, and she had to play the eye contact game to show him who was boss.

"You think you can do whatever you want because you have a house and a push over husband? Well let me tell you something, *Thunderthighs*. You ain't *shit*. Just because your daddy got you a fancy job on TV, doesn't mean you're better than me!"

She had to give it to Freddie; he had a hidden talent of knowing exactly how to hurt someone. He could read a person and excavate their hidden insecurities within a matter of seconds. Then he strung together all the insults in a way that would push the knife in even deeper. Even though *Thunderthighs* didn't sting as hard as it had eleven years ago, the way that Freddie integrated it into the sentence made her want to smack him across the face. Furthermore, the jab about her getting her job because of her 'daddy' made her face turn red with anger. It was true that her dad had pulled some strings for her in Boston, but she had gotten her job in Birkbridge without any help from her father. She landed the job fair and square from Jim, who had instantly taken a liking to her. And in exchange for hiring her, Eliza had helped Jim to build an empire out of his measly TV station.

Eliza could feel the vein in her forehead throbbing. Her rage had escalated too far to hide, but she figured that at least she wouldn't show any fear. She wasn't scared of this drug-ridden shell of a man who stood in front of her. This was her house, and he was going to have to leave, pay or no pay.

"Freddie, I'm asking you to leave one more time, and then I'm calling the police," she warned him coldly.

“I’m not leaving until I get paid.”

“Then I don’t have much of a choice.” Eliza calmly walked over to the phone.

“No you don’t, you dirty bitch,” Freddie growled. Before Eliza knew it, she was wrestled onto the ground by Freddie’s bony hands.

“Get off me!” she yelled. Finally, Freddie had achieved what he had wanted all along; he had made her express fear.

Eliza tried to get up, but Freddie’s paws were clawing at her, preventing her from pushing herself back up.

“You fat slut. You think you’re hot shit, don’t you?!”

Freddie managed to push Eliza’s hands onto the ground as she struggled.

“Oh no you don’t, I’ve got you now, bitch. Let’s see how hot you really are…”

As he held her down with one arm, Freddie raised his other hand to Eliza’s blouse and started tugging at it.

Eliza’s soul felt like it was being wrenched from her body. Her entire body felt numb, as if she were being taken over by a foreign spirit. Before she knew it, she was standing with both feet on the ground, looking down at Freddie, who was writhing around on the ground, holding his wrist. His hand looked like it had been subjected to rope burn; the entire circumference was red and raw.

After a moment on the floor, the fire returned to Freddie's eyes and he got up. Eliza ran into the bathroom, and to her relief, remembered that she'd left her phone there just before Freddie came by.

She picked up the phone and immediately saw three missed calls from Hayden. *He must already be waiting for me at the café.* Without thinking, she pressed the call back button. Hayden picked up, his voice calm and dreamy.

Instead of talking, Eliza started to sob. She had been holding in a wide spectrum of emotional distress throughout her ordeal with Freddie, from the moment that he got in the door until the instance where he tried to sexually assault her and she fought him off. As the numbness faded, the flood of emotions caught Eliza off-guard, and she was unable to speak.

"Eliza, what's wrong?" Hayden's voice suddenly had an alertness to it. Eliza felt as if he were reading her mind through the phone. It was as if he was able to sense the heightened danger.

"I…" she began, her words drowning in tears. "Freddie, a man who painted our house, he came over and demanded money. I gave him a check and then he pushed me, and then he tried to rape me!" As she said these words, Eliza's heart felt like it was being ripped out of her body. Her throat was sore, as if she'd just swallowed an oversized apple without chewing it.

Hayden's voice remained leveled, but there was an element of impending danger in the way he spoke. "Are you safe?"

"Yes, I've locked myself in the bathroom."

"Is he still in the house?" Hayden uttered with such sharpness, his words could cut glass.

"I'm not sure but I don't think so. He might've left."

"Ok. Listen to me, Eliza," he said, his tone both stern and comforting at the same time. "No matter what you do, stay in the bathroom. Don't unlock the door for anyone. What is your address?"

Hayden hung up the phone. Eliza put the toilet cover down and sat on it. She stared at her phone for a minute, her thoughts flittering in and out. Eliza had never felt this detached from her own body and mind. It felt as if she had taken on multiple personalities within the past twenty minutes. She didn't even fully understand how she had managed to fight Freddie off. Granted, he was skinny, but he was also a giant, and his arms had been freakishly strong. The memory of the struggle was blurry, but Eliza recalled the way that Freddie had grasped at his wrist as he writhed around on the ground. Her survival instincts must've kicked in during the attack, and she used all the power she had to grab his dirty arm and thrust it away from her blouse.

Time seemed to slow down and speed up for the following ten minutes. Eliza didn't even notice the sound of the back door unlocking as Hayden broke into her house, and she also didn't hear him rummage around, checking all the rooms of her house to make sure that the coast was clear. When he convinced himself that Freddie could not be found, Hayden knocked on the bathroom door. "Eliza, it's Hayden. He's gone, you're safe now. You can come out."

It took a few moments for Eliza to jump out of her trance-like state and register the sound of Hayden's voice. She unlocked the door weakly. Her energy felt completely drained by the fight.

"Hayden, thank you for being here. I'm sorry I missed the coffee…"

Hayden resisted the urge to smile. "Eliza, you're worried about missing out on meeting me for *coffee* during a time like this? You are one tough lady."

Eliza's spirits lifted a little as she looked up at Hayden's face. How could a man who seemed so *edgy* also appear so gentle and caring?

"Come on, let's get you out of here," he told her. "It's not good for you to stay here until we can make sure that this man won't be coming back."

The following half hour was a blur, as Eliza came back slowly to her senses. Hayden drove her to a hotel, where he booked a large suite. "My place in the mines isn't so nice, plus I share a room with my brother. It'll be more relaxing if you get a place with some more space," he told her.

There was a big hot tub in the middle of the large suite, and Hayden ran Eliza a hot bath as soon as they walked in. He ordered some room service, which arrived within seven minutes, precisely at the point when the bath had filled up to the brim.

Eliza looked at him reluctantly, wondering whether he would be here the whole time. She wasn't sure if she felt comfortable about getting in the hot tub while he was there. Just as she was thinking that, she had her answer. Hayden was putting on his coat, which meant he would be going somewhere.

"Stay here for the meantime, call in sick with work. It's not safe for you to be out in case this asshole tries to cover his tracks by doing something drastic."

"Where will you be?"

"I'm going to deal with this man. I'll make sure he never tries to hurt you again."

"Are you sure? I mean… shouldn't we call the police?"

"I don't think that will be necessary," Hayden replied, his smooth voice picking up some hints of darkness.

"Be careful," Eliza said in a worried tone. As soon as those words left her mouth, she felt a little foolish. Freddie could never do anything to Hayden, could he? Unless he called his drug dealing friends… but he probably wouldn't have time for that. Eliza looked at

Hayden, and the expression on his face assured her that he would be just fine.

"Don't worry," he replied with total confidence. "I'll be fine."

Hayden left, promising to return within two or three hours. Eliza texted Jim to tell him she was feeling under the weather. She switched the jet function on in the hot tub and started to peel off her clothes. Eliza stepped into the water gradually, the hot water caressing her body. She allowed herself to submerge completely under water as the bubbles fizzed all around her body. Eliza came up for air and leaned back against the tub.

The strong little bubble-making streams of water tickled her back, her legs and her arms. She took a strawberry from the room service platter and washed it down with a glass of champagne. Now her body and her mind were filled with bubbles. Eliza shifted in the tub and angled her body sideways. The new position made her feel the bubble streams pump onto other parts of her body. One of the particularly strong streams of water was hitting her between the legs, and the sensation was beginning to feel increasingly pleasant.

She leaned her head against the rest, allowing the muscles in her back and shoulders to relax. Eliza began to think about Hayden as the reality of what he was about to do was finally sinking in. *He's about to singlehandedly deal with my attempted rapist.* But what would he do? Give Freddie a speech, rough him up a little? Or would he corner him in an abandoned building, possibly near the mines, and lock him up?

Maybe he'd torture him even, or burn down his house. According to coffee shop gossip and the help of living in a small town, it was widely believed that Freddie kept and sold drugs from his house, so burning it down would certainly teach him a lesson.

Eliza was not malicious or sadistic, but the thought of Hayden fighting for her honor made her body tingle. *He's doing this for me.*

She imagined Hayden coming back to the room after he had dealt with Freddie, with drops of blood on his shirt and a look of victory in his eyes. Eliza would be lying on the bed, waiting for him to return impatiently.

As she visualized this scenario, the strong stream of water massaged her clitoris. The sensation felt so good that her legs began to shake with pleasure. She pictured Hayden ripping off his blood-stained shirt and walking over to the bed, his pace steady and slow. She would look into his wild eyes as he stepped out of his jeans. When he approached the edge of her bed, she would sit up on her knees and caress his taut abdomen. Slowly, she would work her hands down and hook her thumbs over the edges of his underwear, tugging them down gently.

Eliza flipped another switch on the Jacuzzi, and the strength of the bubbles doubled. The strong stream began to pulsate with double the intensity, forcing her to moan with pleasure. She imagined Hayden's strong, toned arms gripping her around the waist as they embraced. He would kiss her neck and work his way down. Eliza felt the intensity build as the water massaged her sensitive area. She thought about her hands all over Hayden's body as she wrapped her legs around his waist. The pleasure grew more intense, and Eliza floated with bliss as she climaxed. As her soul returned to her body, she felt the warm water caress her.

Before getting out of the bath, Eliza opened a tiny shampoo bottle and emptied the contents all over her hair. She used her hands and nails to massage the lather into her long, brown locks. Then she stood up and washed her body with shower gel, taking her time to let the foam caress her skin. After rinsing off, Eliza put on a fresh, fluffy white bathrobe and towel dried her hair. She propped up a few pillows on the bed and leaned against them, picking up the remote to flick through some channels.

By the time that Hayden returned to the hotel, Eliza was fast asleep. He gently picked up the blankets and placed them over her body, and she began to stir. When she opened her eyes, Hayden was sitting at the edge of the bed, watching her with calm eyes. His hair was a little scraggly, but otherwise he looked completely calm.

"Hi," he said as her eyelids came up and her eyes rested on his.

"Are you ok?" Eliza asked, scanning his body for any signs of fighting.

"I'm much better than ok." He smiled. "I felt better the very moment I walked into this room and saw you lying there. You're very pretty when you sleep."

"Thanks," Eliza mumbled bashfully. She wasn't feeling very pretty because her hair was all tangled and frizzy.

"I like your hair like that," Hayden said, his hand coming up to touch it. Once again, it felt like he had read her mind. For a few moments, they sat in silence as he stroked her long, flowing locks. Eliza felt safe, cared for. She closed her eyes and finally felt her thoughts begin to evaporate as she felt more and more at ease.

Hayden kicked off his shoes and lay next to Eliza, taking her hand in his. They lay down for a while, eyes closed but not sleeping.

Chapter Ten

Eliza was already back when Andrew came home from work. She had cooked dinner and attempted to have a bite but the smell of food was making her feel queasy. The only thing she'd had that day was a few strawberries, and it seemed to be all that she could handle.

Andrew entered the living room, his face immediately brightening when he saw the food on the table.

"Did you cook dinner?"

"As a matter of fact, I did," Eliza replied, her mouth twisting up at the corners.

"How come you haven't eaten anything? Were you waiting for me?"

"I wasn't feeling so well today so I took a day off work."

"Oh no, you're sick?" Andrew rushed over to her exaggeratedly. He wrapped his hand around her wrist. "I feel a pulse! I repeat, there is a pulse on this one!"

Eliza laughed, and Andrew gave her a peck on the forehead. He sat down opposite her and began to dig into the food.

For many reasons, Eliza made the decision not to tell Andrew about what really happened that day. It was a difficult decision to make, considering that they never kept secrets from one another. However, she found no feasible way to explain the fact that she had called Hayden instead of the him or the police. Furthermore, Andrew might be prompted to go over and pay Freddie a visit, and she didn't want him to get into any trouble. Unlike Hayden, Andrew was not the type to be discreet or subtle, and she didn't want Andrew to get in trouble with the police.

The following day, Eliza decided to visit her parents after work. Given her current circumstances, there was virtually nobody who she could talk to about her dilemma. She had never felt as emotionally distant from Andrew as she did at this very moment, and she knew that her father would understand what she was going through. After all, her parents' relationship had often been rocky and it seemed to always be her father who had found a way to reconcile their differences when times got tough. Ironically, most of Jeanette and Martin's arguments were technically caused by Martin's actions. Lately, the biggest issue was Martin's historical projects, which kept him busy with research day and night. They also often bordered on obsessive, despite the fact that they didn't bring much money in. Eliza felt as if she was doomed to repeat her father's mistakes, since she was now the one causing the distance in her relationship. Therefore, she knew that she must also be the one to fix things with Andrew, and she was prepared to take her father's advice in order to deal with the situation.

Jeanette greeted Eliza at the door, smiling from ear to ear. "Darling! I am so happy to see you!"

Since Jeanette had learned to speak English from watching classic, black and white movies, her manner of speech was an interesting combination of influences. Her Italian accent was intertwined with some hints of American and British expressions, adopted from films like *My Fair Lady* and *All About Eve*. The most Italian thing about her speech was the way that she dragged her vowels and emphasized her consonants. Eliza's mother never lacked energy in her presence, and she always felt the need to speak her mind.

"I've missed you, too, Jean," Eliza said, giving her mother a hug.

Ever since she was a child, Eliza had referred to her parents by their first names. It wasn't a symptom of coldness or parental disassociation, but simply a matter of habit. Her parents had always called each other by name, and she had followed suit. She'd learned the words "Martin" and "Jean" before she learned "Mom" and "Dad", hence the former words were the ones that stuck.

Jeanette kept chattering on as she ushered her daughter into the house. "You look more and more like your father every day. The only thing Italian about you is your hair!"

"Well, I'm really grateful for the hair, Jean. It's a nightmare to brush every morning, but I wouldn't trade it for anything."

"Oh, of course. I just wish that there was more of me in you, my dear. You have your father's career, your father's good looks, your father's temperament…"

At this point, Martin walked through the door. "She has both of our eyes," he said, his voice warm and cool at the same time.

"You both have green eyes," Jeanette insisted.

"Yes, but they look like yours," Martin said, approaching his wife and touching her hair gently. Jeanette looked a little embarrassed and shrugged his hand away.

"I'll get some food ready," she said, her voice getting slightly shrill and flustered. She scurried off into the kitchen, leaving Eliza alone with her father.

"I'm sorry about that," he said. "Your mother and I have been having a lot of misunderstandings lately."

"I understand."

"Come on, let's go to my study. There's something that I was meaning to show you."

They walked into the study, and as soon as the door shut, Martin started talking. His usually steady voice was revealing hints of excitement. "I think I've made a breakthrough in my research."

Eliza cocked her head to the side. Martin's research was typically not the type to have any 'breakthroughs'.

"Oh? What did you find out?" she asked supportively, attempting to hide her skepticism.

"Well, that's the thing. I'm not quite sure."

Eliza looked at her father without saying much. Had the multitudes of consecutive hours that he had spent locked up in an office finally driven him mad?

"Let me explain," he continued, amused by his daughter's obvious hesitation. Even though Eliza had inherited her father's temperament, she had taken after her mother in certain expressive giveaways. Her face was often unable to hide emotions, which was beneficial for reading tragic newscasts but very bad for playing poker.

"You know how I've been researching the history of Millstone Firearms?"

"Yes…" Eliza replied. She was a little bit too aware about her father's frequent visits to the factory. Even though Andrew was careful not to mention it, his colleagues would often bring it up when she ran into them at the *Beer Cave*. Alongside her disdain for playing pool, this had been another reason that she had stopped frequenting the venue in recent months.

"Well," he continued, "so far my research has been completely linear, and I was tracing the history of Millstone, dating almost 100 years back. But in the past week, as I was speaking to a new warehouse worker, I found out that Millhouse had increased their staff by almost five percent within the past *week*. The new guy told me that they were still hiring. Do you know if this is true?"

"Yes, I know Andrew's been interviewing personnel for management level positions as well. But I don't see how this is relevant…"

"You will in a second. The thing is, until now, I hadn't noticed any solid *patterns* in the way that Millstone Firearms has operated, since none of the figures had any recurring properties. Or so I thought…"

"Ok, so you found a pattern in the hirings and firings?"

"Not within the company itself, no."

"Well then what did you —"

"I compared the data to the figures of another major company in Birkbridge," Martin interrupted, unable to contain his excitement any longer. "The fact that I made the connection was pure coincidence, since I happened to hear that the mines also hired a large number of personnel in the past couple of weeks."

Martin picked up a thermal mug from his desk and took a sip. "Then, without going deep into research, I pulled up some figures that I found online. It was all up there, in plain sight. It turns out that there is a pattern; not within the individual industries, but *between* them. For the past 100 years, the personnel figures within both companies have risen and declined almost simultaneously. They would rise steadily, and then after a couple of months after the intensive hiring process, they would decline."

"Couldn't it just be that the two industries were reacting to one another competitively, but after expanding their workforce they simply didn't have enough resources to sustain them, forcing them to fire people?" Eliza offered.

"I'm not too sure. My gut tells me that something else is up, but I haven't made the connection yet. Also, industries are rarely susceptible to competing with one another unless their products are somehow related. However, you might be right; we live in a small town, with only three main industries; agriculture, mining and weapons. Agriculture is a stable industry, while the other two are open to fluctuations. So maybe they are competing over being the town's main exports, since resources are relatively limited. Maybe they wanted to snatch up all the able personnel in the nearby towns before the other company could get to them."

"That's also possible…" Eliza responded, her tone still suggesting that she was unconvinced by her father's 'big breakthrough'. As always, her father could read her like an open book.

"I like the way you think, Ellie. You're very logical and you don't take any information lightly without checking the facts. But this is why I wanted to ask you a favor. Maybe you can do some of your own investigating. Not that I'd like you to pry, but merely try and take *interest* in what Andrew is doing. Ask him how the new recruitment process is going, and maybe ask him some 'why' questions; nothing major. Possibly, you could also ask your boss whether he's picked up on anything. Jim has excellent radar for current events, so he might have a little bit of insight into the recent developments in the mines."

"Sure, I don't mind doing that," Eliza agreed. She would do anything to help her father, but she was also a little worried about this new project of his. It was not unlike her father to be absorbed by his work, but she'd also never heard him speak about making 'breakthroughs'. She was a little worried that he might be disappointed if he found that the real cause of the coinciding patterns was anything less than extraordinary.

Martin looked relieved. "I appreciate it, Ellie. You're busy these days and you have your own life, so I appreciate you coming down and listening to your old father about his crazy delusional ideas."

Eliza laughed. "Please, Martin. You might be crazy, but you're not old. Well, maybe you're old but you don't *look* old. In fact, you look young enough to pass for my brother!"

Martin chuckled and put a finger to his lips. "Shhh… don't tell your mother that. She gets jealous."

"I know, Dad. Speaking of which, I wanted to ask your advice on something. Andrew and I have always been really good together, and I think it's because we're usually very honest with one another. And I still try to be, but we've been together for a long time, and I guess it's inevitable that there are certain things that I simply haven't been able to share with him. It's strange for me because I'm not used to keeping things from him, but I felt like I had no choice. Now I'm concerned that there's this space growing between us, and I need to find a way to stop it from expanding. Sorry if this sounds melodramatic."

"Ellie, you don't have to feel guilty for admitting that your relationship isn't perfect. Nobody's is."

"I know that. I guess that I was a little naïve because I really *did* think that Andrew and I were perfect. But now I'm not so sure. We've been so busy, so when we spend time together it's always great. Now I'm beginning to think that I was mistaking our reluctance to have real conversations with a perfect relationship. We never bring up any real concerns or nag at one another, so it's created the illusion that nothing is wrong."

Eliza only now began to realize that her reluctance to confront Andrew came from her deep-seated fear of becoming like her mother. She fashioned herself as the cool girlfriend; the one who never complained when her boyfriend stayed late playing pool and drinking beer with his friends. She wanted to be the girlfriend who never flustered or nagged, and Eliza was proud that she had managed to keep her cool about so many things.

"Look, sweetheart. I know that you're worried, and that your mother and I don't provide the most perfect example of an adult relationship. But you have to remember that this man of yours loves you, and that he won't stop caring for you just because you told him to take out the trash or come home early, or spend some time hanging out with you and your friends. All you have to do is ask, and he'll be there for you. I think that you're feeling the gap grow because the more that you refuse to confront him about something, the more you're driven to shut yourself in. I know because that's how I react in these situations."

Eliza nodded in agreement. She was glad that her father understood her situation, and his words were making a lot of sense.

"You shouldn't feel guilty about anything you did or didn't tell him in the past," her father assured her. "Just try to break the cycle of silence, and next time something's on your mind, don't be afraid to bring it up. Andrew will listen to you, no matter what you have to say."

"Thanks, this has actually been really helpful."

"What did you expect? This old man also knows a thing or two about life."

Eliza went into the kitchen and helped her mother set the table. They ate dinner in the same way as always; Martin and Eliza listened while Jeanette talked. After a while, she finally managed to push Eliza into talking about her work, and Eliza took this opportunity to complain about Jim and his sudden descent into lameness. Her mother seemed animated by this news, and started suggesting that Eliza quit and start her own news station. Eliza smiled politely and cracked a joke.

"Birkbridge isn't ready for the kind of things that I'd like to show them!"

"That's my daughter!" her mother exclaimed proudly.

Martin spooned his vegetables in silence, albeit a comfortable one. His expression was difficult to read as usual, but when Eliza caught a glimpse of her father's eyes, she could tell that he was content. Content was good; ever since Eliza could remember, this was the closest that Martin could ever get to happiness.

After dinner, Eliza still had one more place that she needed to go to. She met Melissa at their usual table at *Nelly's*, but this time without Brienne. Melissa had texted her and said that there was something important they needed to discuss, and Eliza was pretty sure that it involved Theo.

Melissa walked in, looking as flustered as she had when they met for their first double date that weekend. Eliza felt as if they were both riding a roller coaster of ups and downs. Every time something went right, something else would go terribly wrong. Even though Melissa had met the man of her dreams, her troubles were not even close to being over.

By the time Melissa came in, there was already a drink ready on her side of the table. This cheered her up a bit. "Thanks, El!" she said. "Sorry for calling you on such short notice. I know that you were at your parents' house. I hope you didn't have to leave early because of me…"

"You don't have to thank me, honestly," Eliza told her friend. "You would do the same for me."

Melissa smiled tiredly in response. She took a big sip of her drink and inhaled. Eliza could sense that a big speech was coming up.

"Right. So where to begin? You know how I told you the other day that I wanted to introduce Theo to my mom?"

"'Course I remember."

"Ok, so Theo and I decided to visit her yesterday. I called in advance and told her that I'd be coming, and I hinted that I might bring a friend. Of course, she probably thought that I meant *you*, but I decided that it didn't matter, as long as she was prepared for some sort of company."

Melissa took another sip of her drink. "So we arrived, and I spoke to her. We made some tea, had a pretty nice chat. And everything was really good. And by really good, I mean *normal*. There was no mumbo jumbo about how I'm in danger or how I need to do some kind of cleansing ritual before I go to bed or how I should never leave the back door of the house unlocked, even when I'm in."

"That sounds good."

Noticing Eliza's confused expression, Melissa continued. "No, no, but just wait until you hear what happened. You see, I guess all the normality was just too much, so she decided to make up for it by putting on a pretty big show.”

“I see… I’m sorry to hear that. Did you get to introduce her to Theo nonetheless?”

“Well, yes, because the outburst happened *after* she met Theo.”

Eliza finally began to picture what must’ve happened. “Ooh. I see.”

“Uhum,” Melissa nodded, picking up that Eliza was finally on the same wavelength. “So everything was going so great, and I told her that I had a friend with me, and that he was a man. I expected her to freak out, but she just nodded and asked if he wanted to join us for tea. So I went and fetched Theo, who was sitting in the reception area. You should’ve seen him, sitting there reading a magazine, acting totally oblivious to the fact that *everybody* was staring at him.”

Melissa noticed herself digressing as she swooned over the memory of Theo’s gorgeousness. “So anyway, we come back to the room and make the introductions, and we’re all drinking tea. Then Naomi looks at Theo’s tea, and I guess she thought she was doing some sort of tea-leaf reading. Next thing we know, she goes into this trance.”

Melissa paused to imitate the wide-eyed stare that her mother exhibited. She took another sip of her drink, finishing it this time.

"Did she just shut off or did she say something?"
Eliza inquired.

"Oh, you bet she said something. She looked
straight at Theo, but her eyes were dead. You know,
like someone who's sleepwalking; they're looking at
you but they're not *seeing* you. So she looks at him and
starts speaking in this deep, croaky voice. I was too
stunned to remember it all properly, but the general take
away from it all was that Theo is the devil."

Melissa paused, her eyes flitting around as she
scanned her mind for the memory. "Oh yeah, she called
him 'an unholy creation' and a 'helper of the devil',
after which she snapped back to normality. She just sat
there drinking her tea, as if nothing had happened! Of
course I was cross, but I couldn't just speak my mind…
not in front of Theo, who, by the way, was handling the
situation extremely well."

"So you don't think your mother was really in a
trance?"

"Well, her mind was definitely in a different place,
but it wasn't an actual trance. She doesn't have a
history of narcolepsy or even sleep talking, and people
don't just jolt into trances."

"You said she looked at the tea leaves. Maybe she
saw a shape that triggered something, maybe a
traumatic memory that made her act out that way. And
since Theo was sitting in front of the cup, her mind
made a connection between him and the traumatic
memory."

"Yes, or she was just trying to freak me out. Or to freak *Theo* out, for that matter. It could all be a front, you know? Her acting so cool at first, and then going completely crazy on us. I thought that she might want me to find someone, settle down and be happy. But I guess she still sees me as a little girl, someone who can't be trusted to make her own decisions."

Eliza didn't know how to respond. On the one hand, she thought that Melissa's sensitive attitude toward her mother might be blocking her from exploring alternative viewpoints. Perhaps Naomi wasn't deliberately trying to sabotage her daughter's happiness; maybe she really thought that she was psychic. Melissa seemed to be convinced that her mother was in the mental health ward by choice rather than by necessity, but Eliza suspected that this wasn't completely true. Objectively speaking, Eliza realized that if Naomi was fully healed, then she wouldn't still be living under care.

On the other hand, Eliza knew that Melissa wasn't prepared to hear the truth. Perhaps she needed to think that her mother wasn't seriously ill in order to get on with her life. Therefore, Eliza had to be careful not to suggest that Naomi had really believed that she was a prophet.

Eliza decided to go with the approach of listening rather than talking. "Melissa, I'm really sorry that the meeting with your mother turned out so badly. Did you and Theo get to speak about what happened?"

"Yeah, and he was obviously really sweet about it, which just made me feel even guiltier. He wanted to spend the night together but I just needed to talk to someone about what happened. It means a lot to me that you came out to listen to me yap on for so long. Tell me about what you've been up to. Has Hayden still been pining after you?"

"No," Eliza shrugged, "we were meant to talk at some point but that fell through."

"Oh, ok. It's probably for the best, even if he wanted to be friends, I can imagine Andrew wouldn't be too thrilled about the prospect of you hanging out with some handsome stranger."

"Right, exactly."

"Anything else up with you? How's work?"

"Work's pretty lame to be honest. You've seen the stuff they make us do lately, running around with prize winning goats and all that nonsense. Nothing much is up otherwise, I went to see my parents, which was nice. They're both so different though, it strikes me as weird every time. I've got a bit of both my parents in me, so I'm a pretty good buffer. I can't even imagine how they can sit at the same table without me around. I feel a bit bad about it sometimes actually."

"Tell me about it! Parents…"

"Yep, it's never easy," Eliza laughed.

Melissa smiled, too. "And that's why we drink."

"I'll drink to that!"

Melissa was looking relieved from managing to talk the whole thing out. They called it an early night and headed home.

<<<>>>

Eliza went to work the next day feeling a little bit more like herself. She regretted not telling Melissa about what had happened to her with Freddie and Hayden, but she knew that Melissa already had a lot on her plate. Nevertheless, speaking to her father had made Eliza feel a bit more positive about her situation with Andrew. Granted, her parents weren't the best example of a happy couple. However, she knew that if they had managed to still live in the same house despite their many differences, then she and Andrew definitely had a good chance of getting over the hump.

Eliza's lighthearted disposition was shattered the moment that she walked into the briefing room. Her eyes immediately landed on the main headline that she would be covering that day.

Local man, Freddie Dormund, found dead in local forest.

Chapter Eleven

Eliza sat with glazed eyes in the briefing room as it filled up with the other members of the team. Oliver sat next to her. He offered her a doughnut and Eliza politely shook her head; her stomach was doing summersaults and she couldn't think about eating. As the crew piled in, an excited buzz filled the room; everyone speculated about the headline of the day. Some people got out their smartphones and began researching the story, but it seemed to not have been covered yet. Eliza realized that their news station might be the first to get the scoop on this story. Perhaps Jim had pulled some strings with the police department. He certainly had his ways.

It felt like hours had passed until Jim finally walked into the room, even though it had only really been a matter of minutes. As he approached the projector, he had a spring in his step and a grin on his face. Judging by his bouncy attitude and slightly disheveled appearance, Eliza guessed that his happiness was about more than just progress at work.

"Well, looks like we have a big story today!" he began.

The hum of the room quietened down and everyone gave Jim their full attention. This was the sort of story that everyone had secretly been waiting for all of these weeks, and finally the universe had presented them with it. Nevertheless, the majority of people in the room kept their faces steady and somber, hiding their excitement.

"So, first things first. Freddie's body was found late last night, and the autopsy is now underway. Therefore, the cause of death hasn't officially been determined yet."

The tension in the room seemed to increase. It was clear that everyone was bursting with questions. Jim, as the entertainment master that he was, kept silent for just long enough to stretch the anticipation. Then he continued.

"*However*, the on-site detectives determined that the *most likely* cause of death was an animal attack. Probably wolves, but this has yet to be confirmed. Statistically, it's highly unlikely, since there are no actual confirmed wolves living in the wild in Indiana."

There was a stir in the room. Oliver turned to Eliza to try and make eye contact but she averted his gaze. Her expressive face had to be controlled as much as possible, and she knew that eye contact would put her at risk of exposure. There were simply too many thoughts running through her mind; she wasn't sure whether to be happy or upset about the cause of death. Surely, it was better if Freddie was killed by a dog or a wolf rather than by Hayden. However, her gut told her that this coincidence was too good to be true.

Eliza raised her hand lightly from the table to signify that she wanted to ask something. Normally Jim would wait until the end of a briefing to answer questions, but Eliza knew that he wouldn't reject her.

Jim seemed surprised at her obvious impatience, but turned to face her nevertheless. "Yes, Eliza?"

"Have the investigators provided any estimates for how long the body was left in the forest until it was found?"

"Good question. Of course, we can't give out any solid facts before the autopsy is complete, but judging purely by the condition of the body, they said it was probably left there for more than one night, but no more than three.

"Thanks, Jim."

Shit. Hayden went to speak with Freddie two days ago, so this aligns with the amount of time that the body must've been in the forest. But if Hayden was behind this, how would he have coordinated an animal attack? Maybe he has connections to somebody who owns vicious dogs? It's certainly the easiest way to cover his tracks...

Eliza was about to ask another question, but she didn't want to draw any suspicion. She just hoped to God that nobody had seen Freddie come to her house two days ago.

Luckily, someone else was thinking along the same lines as her. Rachel raised her hand as well and Jim reluctantly nodded at her.

"Are they investigating any possibilities that this could've been a murder? Given Freddie's reputation, it's easy to believe that he has made some enemies. Perhaps a feud over drug money?"

Jim shot Rachel an irritated look. One question, he could handle; two was pushing it. "They won't know until the autopsy is complete," he snapped.

After Jim finished his briefing, he took Eliza aside to prep her individually. As usual, she was going to be the on-site reporter, meaning that she would be heading into the forest with Oliver and the rest of the camera crew.

"So I hope you're prepared for a bloody one. It's a fresh crime scene, but I know you can handle it. See, you wanted a story like this and finally we got one! I know you'll kick ass. Remember, even though Freddie was a junkie and a dealer, I think that our viewers are craving a positive spin. I know that this guy was beginning to make a living the honest way, doing construction jobs and such."

"I know, he actually did a one-day painting job at my place during the weekend," Eliza said glumly.

"Oh, dear, I'm sorry. This must be so strange for you; having seen him less than a week ago, and now he's dead."

"I know," Eliza sighed. "Don't worry about me though, I'm fine. Tell me about the story."

Jim looked relieved to get the green light for continuing to talk. "Ok, so I was thinking… we can go for the recovering addict angle. A man who was about to make things right, when his past came back to haunt him. No matter whether it was murder or whether he got himself into this trouble, we can still spin it as some kind of karmic retribution for his past deeds. But through his suffering, he's absolved of his sins, and he's in heaven."

"Sounds good," Eliza confirmed.

There was a silence, and Jim glanced up at her. "What? What is it?"

"It's nothing."

"No, Eliza, I can tell that something's on your mind. Just say it."

"Well, between me and you... do you really think this could be a wolf attack? You said it was statistically improbable, so like, what are the chances that it really happened?"

Jim looked thoughtful. "Well… statistically speaking, the last time that there was a wolf attack was over twenty years ago. So it's rare, that's all. Doesn't mean it's impossible."

"Was it exactly twenty years ago?" Eliza confirmed.

"No, I think it was just over that… I should probably double check. Keep getting distracted because I have to keep calling the goddamn morgue and their autopsy people."

"Pathologists," Eliza corrected.

"Exactly. They should be getting back to me anytime now. Excuse me… I'll need to make one more call."

Jim walked off. He was a jumble of excitement and frustration, and despite her anxious state of mind, Eliza still felt some joy in seeing him this way. Finally, the Jim she knew and loved was back.

By the time that the broadcast was ready to begin, it was already 5:30 in the evening. The darkening skies gave the scene an eerie feel, which was ultimately completed by the noticeably large traces of blood that were still on the ground. There was TV-style crime scene investigation tape drawn over the ground. In fact, the whole place felt a bit surreal… like it was crafted for a movie set.

The day was surprisingly calm for November, and Eliza got away with sporting a light jacket. She pushed her shoulders back, held her head high and raised the mike up to her lips. Oliver held up three fingers, then two, then one.

"It is with deep regret that I must announce an untimely death in our community. A local man known as Freddie Dormund, 27, was found dead today, right here in Pinewood Forest."

She paused for a moment and allowed her tone to change from factual to empathetic. It was strange; Eliza was so bad at faking her emotions in life, but in front of the camera, she was the world's greatest actress. Her trick was to allow other emotions to influence her tone. At this moment, she allowed her concern for Hayden's fate into her speech, in order to fake her sympathy for Freddie.

"Freddie was a beloved member of the community, and despite his recent mishaps with the law, he has been on a steady path to recovery from his former addictions. In recent months, Freddie had shown the will to improve his health, his career and his relationships."

Once more, Eliza switched her tone. She looked straight into the camera and allowed her eyes to well up with just enough water to let them glisten, but not enough to cry.

"In fact, Freddie came to work for me just this weekend, and did a wonderful job of painting the outside of my house. His hard work only goes to show that Freddie was serious about making a new life for himself. It is therefore an even greater tragedy that his untimely death coincided with his road to recovery."

Eliza paused again, this time turning away from the camera and touching her right hand to her ear.

"I have just received information that the autopsy reports are back."

She raised up one finger to the camera in order to signify that she was listening to her earpiece. The short wait was good for live TV because it prolonged the audience's anticipation. Eliza was beginning to feel uplifted by her put-on persona and this gave her the willpower to push forward.

She looked back at the camera, her tone serious and sharp. "Our source tells us that the autopsy has revealed that Freddie passed away two days ago. The autopsy has also confirmed that Freddie Dormund has died as a consequence of fatal wounds from a wolf attack."

Eliza paused again as she listened to Jim's voice in her earpiece, and repeated his words into the camera. "The last time that a wolf attack occurred in Birkbridge was in 1994. The police department will issue a statement tonight about the details of the attack and will give an official warning for appropriate conduct. The police chief is currently working on a plan to ensure the safety of our citizens. In the meantime, it is advised that all residents stay away from the forest areas, particularly from Pinewood Forest. An open vigil will be held outside of Mr. Dormund's house tomorrow evening at six. Everyone who wants to pay their respects is welcome."

After rounding off the broadcast, Eliza decided to go straight home. She knew that Jim would probably want her at the office, but she was also aware that he would want to have a lengthy conversation with her about the awesomeness of the broadcast. The show that day really did blow everything else they had done in the past year out of the water. She decided to text him with an excuse about how the blood on the scene had made her queasy. This was half true; not because Eliza was afraid of blood, but because she knew who it belonged to. Her attempted rapist was dead, and she had been the one to report about it. Was this just the irony of life or was there something more to it? After being a reporter for five years, Eliza did not believe in coincidences. There was some missing link between her, Hayden, Freddie and the wolf attack, but she couldn't seem to find it.

On top of all this, there was another uncomfortable piece of information that was now clawing at the back of Eliza's mind. It was something that Jim had said into her earpiece during the broadcast. However, despite the niggling feeling at the back of her mind, Eliza couldn't excavate what it was in particular that bothered her. There were so many other things on her mind at the moment that she couldn't find what it was in particular that had struck her as odd.

Eliza decided that after getting a change of clothes at home, she needed to go see Hayden. The reward of getting closer to the truth of what had happened would be greater than being alone with a potential killer. Her gut told her not to worry, and Eliza had never regretted trusting her intuition. After all, her aversion to Freddie turned out to be completely justified. She simply didn't feel as if she were in any danger with Hayden, despite the fact that he could easily be dangerous. In fact, the dangerous aspect was what drew her toward him in the first place. She somehow knew that he was capable of hurting other people, but she knew that he would never hurt her. And the way that he had rescued her the day that Freddie attacked her only went to show that he would protect her no matter what.

During the drive home, Eliza's phone rang. Andrew's voice came out of the speaker, and she could detect the beer in his tone. Andrew never got completely drunk; he was a big guy and he knew how to pace himself. But he was also not one to hold back on beer night with the boys. She pictured him at the *Beer Cave*, sitting with his friends and watching tonight's broadcast. He would've pointed at the screen, leaning back slightly on his stool as the intoxication set in, and said, "That's my girlfriend!" as if everyone didn't already know.

"Hey, sweetie! Amazing job today, wow, but wow, I mean I can't believe Freddie died." Andrew paused and she heard him taking a drag of a cigarette. He knew she didn't like him smoking every time he drank, but he did it anyway. "I guess he had it coming for being such an a-hole," Andrew whispered. "But no, I don't mean that. It still sucks."

She heard the bar stool move. Even though she could barely make out the sound of Tom's voice, she didn't know what he had shouted. Andrew shouted something back that sounded like, "Yeah, thanks, man, I will!"

"Hey, are you there still? Sorry, had to move to a quieter place."

"I'm still here."

"Oh, ok good. Tom says congratulations, by the way."

"Thanks."

"Listen, did you want to celebrate? I could get out of here now. I've had a bit to drink but I could get a cab. And Tom even said he could drive me home. He's not drunk."

Eliza could tell that Andrew didn't really want to leave the bar, which was all for the best since she needed to see Hayden anyway. "It's ok, sweetie, I actually promised to go see Melissa tonight."

"Ok then, are you sure?"

"Of course, we have a lot of stuff to talk about. She has some stuff going on, family stuff."

"All right then, beautiful, I understand. See you at home, ok? I love you."

"Love you."

Eliza hung up and felt the car go silent. She jogged from her car, now parked in her driveway, to the front door for no particular reason. After the attack, she didn't feel completely comfortable outside of her own home.

She decided to take a much needed shower in order to clear her head. Despite the lengthy conversations that Eliza had with herself in the car, she could still feel that *something* was bothering her. As she soaped her hair and massaged her scalp with her fingers, she could feel that the hidden fact was at the tip of her tongue. *What did we say during the broadcast that was so important?*

At that moment, Eliza realized that she could re-watch the program online. Ever since Jim's network had expanded, he had hired a team of young people. Their sole purpose at the company was to establish an online presence; and they had succeeded marvelously. This meant that every single show was uploaded onto the Internet, almost directly after it aired in real-time. This allowed loyal viewers to catch up on any missed broadcasts immediately, without having to wait to watch the re-runs in the morning. Jim, who came from humble beginnings, believed that traditional TV schedules were a thing of the past. News should be accessible for anyone.

Eliza rinsed herself hurriedly without bothering to untangle her locks in the process, threw on a towel and staggered over to her laptop. She went on the Birkbridge Newsline website and, as always, the team of yuppie geeks had proven themselves worthy of their jobs. The broadcast was online.

She let the video load for a few moments and hit play. Eliza watched herself on the screen. She looked different than usual. There seemed to be a newfound confidence in her stance and an indecipherable look in her eyes. She barely recognized the person she was looking at. Clearly, the past week had had a greater impact on Eliza than she had even realized.

Still, she couldn't figure out what had bothered her. The voice from the laptop continued speaking in its tough, powerful manner. "…the autopsy has also *confirmed* that Freddie Dormund has died as a consequence of fatal wounds from a wolf attack. The last time that a wolf attack occurred in Birkbridge was in 1994. The police department will issue a statement tonight..."

Eliza hit pause. There it was! 1994. That date; that was what had bothered her. But why? She took a moment to think. 1994 was… twenty-three years ago. Why did that date seem so important?

Then it hit her. Her father had spoken to her the day before about his research. Eliza remembered that he believed he'd made a breakthrough because he noticed a pattern in the hirings and firings of the Birkbridge mines and Millstone Firearms. He had told her that twenty-three years ago, both organizations had hired vast numbers of personnel.

But how could this have anything to do with wolf attacks? Suddenly, the coincidences were becoming unbearable. Freddie was killed by a wolf on the same day that he tried to rape her. The last wolf attack in their town had occurred in the same year that her father was investigating to be the peak of expansion in two major local industries.

Eliza realized that she would never be able to find the missing puzzle pieces without doing some research. Even though her father insisted on the importance of field research, her experience in journalism proved that the Internet could be an effective source for a quick fix of information.

She clicked open a new tab and started typing into the search bar: *1994 Birkbridge wolf attack.*

Eliza scrolled down until she found a headline that satisfied her. It read *Married couple killed in wolf attack while visiting Birkbridge, Indiana.* She clicked on the story and began to read. Under the main headline, the subtext read *Husband and wife killed during hike in the forest, leaving behind two sons.*

She read the entire article, which detailed the story of a young couple who travelled to Birkbridge with their sons for a vacation. The parents had gotten up early one morning and ventured into the forest for a stroll, leaving their two boys to sleep in the camper. The parents were found dead four hours later, with bite marks over their body. Eliza noticed that, strangely enough, they had been found by none other than Andrew's father, who had told the police that he had heard 'strange sounds' while hiking in the woods. Apparently, he ran in the direction of the noise and, surely enough, had found two dead bodies that were still warm from the life that had just left them. *Andrew's father. Yet another coincidence*, she thought without enthusiasm.

The children were seven and eight years old at the time. Eliza scrolled down and saw a picture of them, but the caption didn't feature their names. The two boys appeared mischievous and angelic at the same time; they looked as if they'd come straight out of a children's fashion catalogue. Since the article was photocopied entirely from an old newspaper, the photo was black and white. Nevertheless, it was clear that the younger boy's hair and features were lighter than his brother. Even though one was older than the other, they were still the same height. They reminded Eliza of…

Chapter Twelve

Eliza almost choked at the realization she was about to make. *It can't be.* Eliza thought she might be going insane. Perhaps it was through her father's influence that she began to make connections between things that had nothing to do with one another. *But that really looks like them...* She set aside the coincidences for a moment and tried to force herself to look at the photo objectively. Even though it was such an old picture, the resemblance was uncanny. *Hayden and Theo.* She couldn't get these names out of her mind. *Hayden and Theo.* The ages matched too; if Hayden and Theo were seven and eight years old twenty-three years ago, this would make them thirty and thirty-one. This seemed right. Logically, Eliza knew that all of this was too farfetched, but deep down, it all fit perfectly together. She had found one of the missing puzzle pieces.

Eliza pressed 'print,' and watched the pages slowly glide out of the machine. They looked glossy and felt warm to the touch. After jumping out of her trance, Eliza snapped back to reality. Without giving herself time to change her mind, she got dressed, shoved the papers into her bag and rushed into her car. She checked her phone and noticed three missed calls from her father. *This will have to wait.* Eliza would speak to her father after she had sorted this out. There was something incredibly big going on, and she refused to rest until she figured it out.

Eliza turned the ignition and, before she knew it, she was speeding toward the mines. She didn't know exactly where Hayden and Theo lived, so she would have to search their names in the living directory. While driving, she decided to check on Melissa. She called her up on speakerphone, but the only response she received was the low dialing tone of an unanswered phone. She hung up and re-dialed, but there was no luck.

Next, she dialed Hayden's number. She knew that it was best to confront him in person, but she figured that it might be good to give him a heads up that she was driving over.

Hayden picked up after three rings. His voice was calm and smooth on the surface, but Eliza could sense his heightened sense of danger. After all, the last time that Eliza had called him, she had just survived an assault.

"Eliza?"

"Yes. Hi, Hayden." Her heart was racing and her voice came through in broken-up breaths. She sounded as if she'd just been running.

"Is everything all right?"

"Yes, yes." The sounds coming from her mouth were becoming involuntarily high-pitched. She knew that Hayden would suspect something was up, but she refused to say anything until they reunited. "Are you home?"

"Yes, I just finished my evening shift at work. Are you sure everything's ok? Where are you now?"

"I'm actually on my way to see you," Eliza said.

"Eliza…"

"It's ok, I'm already halfway there. Just tell me your cabin number so I don't have to search the directory."

"Thirty-seven."

"Ok, I'll be there in fifteen minutes." She hung up before he could protest.

<<<>>>

Hayden opened the door, and he was a vision to behold. His dark hair was dripping and he wore a towel around his waist.

"You didn't give me much of a warning," he chuckled. "I had to get myself cleaned up… my job is a filthy one."

"It's ok," Eliza said softly. "Can we talk?"

"Sure." Hayden didn't reveal any signs of confusion, but Eliza knew that he must have sensed that something was up. There was something about the way that Hayden looked at her that made her feel as if he could read her mind.

Without further ado, she pulled the printed papers out of her handbag. She passed them to Hayden and watched his face as he read over them. He showed no visible signs of emotion.

"These were your parents," she stated bluntly, scolding herself internally for the unceremonious approach to the topic. She wanted to show more empathy, but Hayden seemed too tough to pity.

Hayden nodded. "Yes, this is Theo and I. Twenty-three years ago, I believe."

"I'm very sorry that this happened to you," she said. "It's unbelievable that you and your brother had to lose your family."

Hayden smiled eerily. "It's all right, we still have family. A very big family, in fact. Almost as big as your boyfriend's, if not bigger."

Eliza paused to consider how Hayden knew about Andrew's family, but realized that he must have done some research. It was no secret that Andrew came from the oldest and biggest family in their small town.

"Do you still see them?" she asked.

"At the annual get togethers, remember?"

Eliza recalled the 'secret location' gatherings that Theo and Hayden had told them about over dinner. "Oh right, the unknown location meetings."

"Not entirely unknown." He smiled. "We decided on this year's location already."

"Oh? Where is it going to be?"

"Right here, actually. In Birkbridge."

"I see. To commemorate your parents?"

"Sort of," he replied, his eyes lighting up with intensity.

There was a silence. Eliza figured that she needed to bring up her question before it was too late. She began slowly. "I'm not sure if you saw my broadcast today…"

"No, sorry, I was working," he replied.

"Right, of course. Well, it turns out that Freddie was killed in the forest two days ago… by wolves."

"Oh?" Once again, Hayden's face revealed a look of amusement, but otherwise didn't expose any other emotion. Eliza knew that she couldn't trick him into a confession, so she would have to ask him upfront.

"Did you have anything to do with this?" she asked, looking deep into his eyes.

"Maybe I did."

Eliza searched her mind for possible explanations, but she was at a loss. "How could you have planned a wolf attack?"

"I don't know…" he said, flashing her a sideways smile. She could tell that he was playing with her. He knew that she was about on the verge of figuring out what had happened, and he was having too much fun to tell her upfront.

"How could it be that the only people to have been killed from a wolf attack in the past twenty-three years are Freddie and your parents? How is that possible?"

"Maybe my parents weren't killed by wolves," he said. "Check your facts."

Eliza looked at the printed article, her eyes flitting around the text, searching for clues.

"Start by checking who found them."

"Alonso Freelander... Andrew's father." As she uttered her boyfriend's name, her voice had shrunk to almost a whisper. The strange coincidences were piling up too thickly to keep track of.

"Well, what do you know about this man?"

"Nothing much, except that he worked at Millstone Firearms for his entire life."

"Exactly. And what was happening at Millstone Firearms during the time that my parents were killed?"

"All I know is that they hired a lot of new personnel," Eliza said, recalling her father's research once more.

"Exactly. And who else was hiring personnel at the time?"

"The mines," Eliza responded, cocking her head slightly. What did any of this have to do with the death of Hayden's parents?

"What if I told you that the rivalry between the mines and the arms factory was about more than just business?"

"I'm listening…"

"Well, would you believe me if I told you that there was a century-old feud between the families that worked for Millstone and the families that worked in the mines?"

"You mean there was a feud between Andrew's family and your family?"

"Yes. And many other families like us."

"What do you mean, *like* you?"

Hayden paused. He looked Eliza in the eyes, as if to confirm that she was ready to hear the truth. She could tell that the game was coming to an end; he was about to tell her the truth.

"I mean, between the families of werewolves, and the families of people who hunt them. And also some *exceptional* people who are caught in between."

Eliza took a moment to process this information. Werewolves? Was she really expected to believe that? But then again, it was hard to come up with any rational explanation for Freddie's untimely death.

"Your parents were killed by werewolves?"

Hayden shook his head, and Eliza realized that she had just misread the situation entirely.

"No. But Freddie was."

Eliza thought about this again. Hayden had suggested that he had been involved in Freddie's death. But if Hayden was a werewolf, then how come his parents were killed by wolves?

"Can you tell me how your parents were killed?"

"Aha! Now you're asking the right questions," he said. "Don't believe everything you read in the papers, Eliza. My parents were killed as the result of trickery. You see, the family of your beloved Andrew was notified of my family's presence in Birkbridge. They didn't see my brother and me as a real threat, since we were not yet showing signs of 'shifting', if you know what I mean. So they targeted my parents."

"But if your parents could shift into wolves, how could Andrew's family get them killed by wolves?"

"This is where things get interesting. The man who orchestrated the murder of my parents, Alonso Freelander, was working on a very important project. He began as a lowly factory worker but his skills qualified him to rise through the ranks fast. Soon afterwards, he became the unofficial supervisor of all the factory workers. This allowed him to quietly designate some resources to his personal project; the development of anti-werewolf weaponry. Werewolves have tough skins that can't be penetrated with ordinary gunfire."

"But your parents weren't killed by guns…" Eliza began. The individual elements of this story didn't seem to be adding up.

"Exactly. This is because, despite Alonso's efforts, his guns were still largely ineffective. He hadn't yet worked out the secret formula. However, he had certain duties to fulfill. You see, like everybody else in his family, Alonso was raised to kill werewolves. In 1994, many of our kind were hired to work in the mines, so Alonso took it upon himself to speed up the hiring process of Millstone Firearms, in order to increase the opposition. Naturally, most of the workers he hired were from his own family. But yes, as it happened, my family was one of the first to arrive in Birkbridge. And at that point, the Millstone boys were ill prepared. Which left Alonso to seek *alternative* measures."

"What kind of measures?"

"Well, he decided to *outsource* the werewolf killing. Like I said earlier, the only two opposing sides are the werewolf families and the hunter families. However, there are also people living amongst us who possess certain faculties that can be useful to both sides. The loyalty of these people can be bought or negotiated, just like with any other professions. And, it just so happened that Alonso had heard of an exceptional young lady who was living in Birkbridge. She was unmarried and had a four-year-old daughter to take care of, so she was a pretty good target for their cause. He hired her, and she was able to use her talents to enter the minds of my parents. First, she hid behind our camper and used her abilities to make them awaken while my brother and I were still sleeping. And then, she lured them into the forest, where Alonso and his family of hunters were waiting. However, Alonso didn't tell the young woman that the hunters' weapons were still useless against werewolves. She walked over to stand by them, thinking that she was safe and that her work was done. She soon realized that *she* was the one who would have to kill the werewolves. Alonso didn't tell her this because he knew she would decline. Naomi was a beautiful young woman who had her entire life ahead of her, and she was not prepared to be a killer."

Eliza looked up at Hayden quizzically, thinking that she had misheard him. "Naomi?"

"Yes, Naomi Lanstead."

Chapter Thirteen

Eliza gulped. Melissa's mother had supernatural abilities? What did this mean for Melissa? And for that matter, what did that mean for Eliza? After all, she was related to Naomi as well.

"What happened to her?" Eliza forced herself to ask.

"Well, after the werewolves saw the armed brigade, they turned. Which means, they took on their animal form. After a short stand-off, they charged, and Naomi realized that the hunters weren't firing their weapons. So, she had to act quickly, and she ended up accessing powers that she didn't even know she possessed. She was able to get into the minds of my parents and set them up against one another. Under the trance she had imposed, they fought each other to death."

Eliza nodded gravely. Andrew's great grandfather had been a master of trickery, and he had played with many lives to achieve his own goals. She didn't quite understand the laws of their family feud, nor could she comprehend the consequences that werewolves and hunters faced for killing their enemies. She now began to understand why Andrew didn't spend much time with his family, and why he had chosen to work in the marketing department rather than the factory. His parents must've told him about the family secret, which Andrew then immediately rejected. Andrew was too kind hearted to participate in a feud with supernatural beings. Deep down, she knew that Hayden was different.

"Did you kill Freddie?" she asked.

Hayden nodded. "I wasn't going to at first, but I learned some things about him when I paid him a visit. I found some… evidence in his house."

"What did you find?"

"Let's just say that you're not the first person this man tried to assault," Hayden replied, his gaze fading into the darkness.

Eliza trusted his judgment; Hayden did not have the look of a sadistic killer. It was strange to her that Andrew's family took it upon themselves to 'protect' the town from werewolves. From her perspective, it seemed that the werewolves had been more kind-hearted to the people of their town than the hunters. After all, she knew firsthand how Melissa's mother had suffered for over twenty years, and now Eliza understood why. She had been tricked into using her supernatural powers to kill two strangers, and was thereafter forced to live with the consequences.

"What about now? If the hunters find out that you've killed, will this spark a feud?"

"I'm not sure. Freddie wasn't a member of their family, so there won't be any revenge killings.

However, if their elders decide that the murder is emblematic of some 'danger' to the town, they might decide to act. I know that their numbers have grown; they've been recruiting as rapidly as the mines to match our numbers. They might not be *planning* an attack, but they're definitely preparing for one."

Eliza stepped closer to Hayden, aware that he was dressed only in a towel. She desperately wished that she could read through his impenetrable gaze. This man had come to her rescue when she was in need, and Eliza wished that she could help to keep him out of danger.

"Is there anything I can do?" she asked him softly. "I can speak to Andrew. He doesn't speak to his family much and I know he's not a hunter; he doesn't even own a gun, but still, maybe there's someone he could talk to. Or I could visit his parents to possibly see if there's anything going on."

Hayden nudged closer to her, his face almost touching hers. Eliza looked up at him, desperately searching for answers in his eyes.

"You don't have to do anything, Eliza. I don't know if I'd be able to forgive myself if you suffered as a consequence of helping me."

Eliza felt a little stung. It made her feel good that Hayden was so protective over her, but it also made her want to scream. Her entire life, she had been waiting for an opportunity to prove that she could deal with immediate danger. She had spent many hours of her childhood watching her father's broadcasts from Afghanistan, and she had always known that she would be doing something similar with her life. It's not that she wanted to risk her life, but she wanted to do something meaningful with it. She wished she could use the strength that she knew she possessed in order to aid other people. And now, here she was, working as a reporter in a town where hardly anything happened, and feeling as if *she* was the one getting rescued all the time. *I'm no damsel in distress.*

"I would really like to help you," she said, leveling her voice and letting it become stern and calm.

Hayden regarded her, his eyes flitting all over her. It appeared that, for once, he was struggling to read her as well. Nevertheless, he kept his cool. Hayden wasn't ready to give up so easily.

"And how would you suggest helping a highly dangerous pack of werewolves?" he asked, lifting an eyebrow. He was challenging her, playing games in order to make her step down. But Eliza was also not a quitter.

"I'm stronger than you think," she said, her voice unfaltering.

"I think I may have underestimated you," Hayden responded.

Eliza didn't say anything, but continued to stare back; shoulders back, neck outstretched. She felt pretty menacing, confident enough to stand up to a werewolf. Werewolf or not, this man had saved her, and she wasn't going to let him pay the price for it.

Hayden's eyes softened and Eliza could see him shed his mask of nonchalance. "Having said that," he continued, "I think you underestimate me in some ways. By that, I mean, I think that you underestimate the things I *say*. But I meant every word, Eliza. When I said that I don't know what I'd do if something bad happened to you, I meant every word." His eyes darkened again, and his voice turned to ice. "I mean that I won't be able to control myself if somebody hurt you. I would hurt them… no, I would kill them. And perhaps there would be others who I'd hurt and possibly kill in the process. I don't want to go into any details about how our kind 'turn', but it might be necessary for you to understand. When we turn, our rage becomes us. This is why my parents couldn't control themselves when Naomi possessed their minds. Once she flipped the switch, all they could feel was rage. And that could happen to me, if something triggered the switch."

"I understand," Eliza told him. She didn't feel the need to explain herself; he would have to trust her judgment.

"You're not scared?" he challenged.

"I told you, I'm not scared of you." Her voice was calm, almost light. She felt at ease with the man standing in front of her, no matter what kind of darkness lurked inside him.

"Oh yeah?"

Eliza nodded at him, refusing to budge. They were still barely an inch away from one another.

"Would you be scared if I did this?" Hayden's voice still had a tinge of darkness in it, and Eliza's heart almost skipped a beat.

He reached his hand out slowly, cupping her chin and pulling her face toward him. His touch was incredibly gentle and soft; Eliza felt like she was a porcelain doll that he was scared of breaking.

Hayden pulled her mouth close to his, and suddenly, he wasn't holding back anymore. As soon as their lips touched, Hayden's desire unfolded like an uncontrollable force. He felt soft at first, but as soon as Eliza surrendered her lips to his, the kiss became almost savage. Hayden pulled away, his eyes ablaze with passion, and he began to kiss her neck, her shoulders, her breasts. Before she knew it, Eliza was lying on the bed, Hayden's strong arms holding her down by the wrists. He looked almost possessed by his desire, but Eliza wasn't frightened; the bulge beneath his towel brushed up against her thigh. At the same time, she felt at the mercy of his strength, but she also felt protected by it. She recalled the night that he came back to the hotel after fighting for her honor; he had looked and sounded like a warrior, but when he sat down on the bed with her and stroked her hair, his touch had been ever so soft.

Eliza's legs began to lightly shake as Hayden kissed her. He hovered over her body, his broad shoulders accentuating his aggressive frame. He looked like a fighter who had returned to his woman after battle and was claiming his long-awaited prize. Of course, Eliza was too tough to think of herself as a prize to be won, but with Hayden, it was different. She felt like he deserved her, just as she deserved him. In Hayden, she had finally met her match.

His body glided over hers as he explored her with his mouth. He worked his way down, and then back up again, concentrating on her breasts and her neck. Hayden pulled back, looking at Eliza with blazing eyes. "Still not scared?"

"With you, I'm not scared of anything." As she said this, Eliza hooked her right leg around Hayden's torso and twisted her body around his. Within a split second, she was straddling him. She wrapped her legs around him and let her hands wander over his bare chest and his firm, lean torso.

Hayden's expression was a mix of admiration and craving desire. The sudden swap of control made him want her even more, but she was tempted to tease him. She kissed his neck and chest as Hayden's hands caressed her waist and her ample behind. "You really do have curves in all the right places," he breathed lustily. Eliza could tell that he craved more, but she wasn't ready to give it to him just yet. She hooked her hand over his towel and worked it loose.

She unbuttoned her own shirt and removed it over her head, throwing it down onto the floor. She met Hayden's smiling eyes and giggled. Laughing felt liberating; she felt carefree and completely at ease. The possibilities seemed endless and the anticipation made things all the more exciting. Slowly, she slid her fingers down his taut abs. It was as if his whole body was an upside down triangle, starting at his broad shoulders and pointing down toward his groin.

She grabbed a corner of his towel and tugged. As she freed his manhood, she shifted her body back onto the bed, leaning forward slightly. While Eliza tossed the towel aside, she snuck a peek at his face. Contrastingly to his usually calm exterior, he now seemed like a bundle of frustration and anticipation. The waiting was driving him crazy, and Eliza fully enjoyed the feeling of power that this gave her.

Eliza smiled at Hayden cheekily and lowered her body even further down. Slowly, she took him in her mouth, exploring his entire length with her tongue. She looked up and saw him close his eyes with pleasure, and she increased the pace. His hands came down to touch her long, flowing hair and she could feel his grip tighten as the pleasure increased.

She came back up and teased him a little, nibbling at the lower regions of his abdomen. She removed her black pants and underwear, and swiftly climbed on top of Hayden's body, her legs wrapping around him. They were both breathing quickly as the intensity escalated, and Eliza was acting with fast, unthinking impulsivity.

Eliza decided to keep her lacy, black bra on to support her D-cups as she swayed on top of Hayden's body. She arched her body back as she grinded on top of him, feeling every inch of his length hitting the sensitive area inside of her. Hayden's hands came out to pull her closer to him, and she leaned her body to meet his. She kept riding him while he kissed her lips passionately, their mouths expressing the escalating pleasure and the desire to climax.

With her body close to his, she could feel the friction begin to increase on her clitoris, which made Eliza move faster. Hayden worked his hips up to meet her movement, increasing the pleasure even more. Meanwhile, Hayden had managed to move the bra cups to the side, allowing him to cup her breasts with his hands. He squeezed at her nipples gently, the delicious pain of which made her want to ride him even faster. Hayden's eyes were opening and closing as he strained to delay the climax. She continued to grind her hips faster and faster, and she could feel him get even harder inside of her as he got ready to explode. Suddenly, Eliza lost all sense of her surroundings; the pleasure escalated into a completely new dimension. The delicious sensation spread all over her body as her pulse rose and her muscles contracted.

Hayden's release matched hers, and their bodies tensed up with intense pleasure before coming back to reality. They lay in bed for a while and Hayden buried his face into Eliza's hair. She gripped his hand tightly when her legs tensed up with little aftershocks. He hugged her close to him, allowing his right hand to glide over her body soothingly.

Eliza didn't feel herself falling asleep, but she woke up in half an hour from the sound of a running shower. She peeled the covers off and reached for her phone, noticing yet another missed phone call from her father. She heard the shower water stop and Hayden emerged, his body looking hard and smooth at the same time.

Eliza reached up to touch him, just to prove to herself that he was real.

And this was when they heard the first gunshot.

Chapter Fourteen

In one swift motion, Hayden stood in front of Eliza, shielding her with his body. For a moment, everything was quiet. Eliza sat on the bed, motionless, and watched as Hayden glanced left and right, checking for bullet holes in the walls. After he made sure that the gunshot had not penetrated their room, he pulled Eliza up and handed her a shirt.

"I need to go outside and see what happened," he told her. "It's up to you whether you want to come or stay."

Eliza didn't need much time to think. She knew that she would go with him. Hayden ran to the closet and emerged with a fresh shirt and jeans. Eliza pulled her pants back on and slid into her shoes. Hayden walked in front of her as he opened the door, carefully shielding her with his broad frame.

The housing complexes in the mines weren't surrounded by many streetlights, but the lights from the neighboring houses provided some extra light for visibility. There were no more gunshots, but the sound of a commotion was audible, and they ran along the street toward it.

As they approached a scattered group of people, Eliza was not at all prepared for what she was about to see. They ran forward for a while, but her sight was blocked by Hayden's body. However, as he moved a little to the side, she managed to catch a glimpse of the man holding the gun.

It was Andrew.

"Andrew!" she yelled at the top of her lungs, her voice cracking with the strain on her vocal chords.

He looked at her without moving his stance. The gun was still aimed in front of him. Eliza kept running until she got close enough to see his face.

"Eliza? What are you doing here?" His voice was filled with concern as he looked from her to Hayden. "Did he try to hurt you?" he shouted accusingly.

"No, he was trying to help me… it's got something to do with Freddie. I'll explain later. What's going on?"

Andrew looked back into the direction where his gun was pointing, and Eliza followed his gaze. She couldn't quite make out what was in front of her; she could see some large, dark bushes, and possibly the face of a man. Hayden walked slowly toward the dark shapes. Eliza squinted her eyes in an attempt to fight the blurriness of night vision. Before she knew it, Hayden was sprinting back to her so fast that his feet were barely touching the ground.

"Eliza! You need to get away. It isn't safe for you here."

"What do you mean? What's going…?"

As she uttered those words, she heard a loud growl coming from the shape in the bushes. The background began to move, and suddenly she realized that the mass she had mistaken for greenery was not a bush at all.

The wolf growled louder, and this time the rage seemed to be directed at her. She stood dead in her tracks, trying to make out the shape of the man who stood in front of it.

"Eliza, you have to go. He won't let go of your father until he feels safe. I'll talk to Andrew, tell him to back down with the guns," Hayden told her as he moved in front of her, shielding her from the werewolf.

Eliza felt light headed. Had she misunderstood him?

"My father?" she asked.

At this point, Andrew turned to face her, his gun still in place. "He's right, Eliza. You need to go. I'll take care of this."

Eliza darted past Hayden in an attempt to get a closer look. Maybe they were mistaken… maybe it was someone else… She squinted her eyes again, and this time she was certain of it. The man who was locked in the werewolf's grip was her father.

"Eliza!" Hayden yelled. Within a split second, he was in front of her again. He picked her up and carried her, placing her down behind Andrew. Then he started running again, sprinting back to the werewolf.

"I wouldn't trust him if I were you," Andrew told Eliza, his eyes still fixated on the werewolf.

"He's trying to help us!" Eliza said, her voice failing to hide her dismay.

"No, I'm trying to help us," Andrew said sternly. "Your father called me earlier, but I was at the bar still and I didn't hear his call. I listened to my voicemail on my way home, and I had a message from your father. He told me he had tried to contact you several times, but without any luck. He said he needed to speak to you about your broadcast… something about 1994. He said that everything made sense now, that his epiphany wasn't misguided after all. Before he finished the message, he mentioned that he might be 'stopping by' the mines to investigate. He made me worry, Eliza, and thank God for that. Because if I hadn't arrived on time, who knows what could've happened?"

"Andrew, what happened? Is Martin hurt?"

"No, but he was about to be. He was in a heated argument with this man, and then he turned. He was about to attack him, Eliza. I shot at him once. I didn't hit him, but the shot helped to distract the wolf's attention from your father. But now, we're in a stalemate. He won't kill him while I have a clean shot of him, but he also won't let him go until I put my weapon down."

"Why can't you put it down?"

"I can't trust their kind. Maybe you only trust that man because he was nice to you once, but don't be fooled. When they turn, everything human in them disappears. In the state he's in, he can't listen to reason; he'll react on impulse. Who is to say that, once I put my weapon down, he won't take Martin's head off in one swift motion?"

Eliza couldn't bear to even register that image. She looked at Andrew's face, and his look of dead seriousness convinced her that he wasn't lying. How did he know so much about werewolves? And for that matter, when had he learned to shoot a gun? She was beginning to realize that the man who she had lived with for four years had a completely different side to him; a side she had not witnessed until now. He even looked different; he stood straight, shoulders back, right hand forward. He wasn't shaking, quivering or moving in any way; Andrew was the picture of quiet, controlled confidence. His whole body was attentive and alert, and Eliza could trust that he would shoot to kill if the werewolf made one move to hurt her father.

Hayden came running back, sweat running down his chest. He walked directly over to Andrew. "He says he'll let go if you put your weapon down!"

"No chance. If I put my weapon down, there's nothing to stop him from going for the kill."

It was clear that Hayden was beginning to lose his cool. Andrew's cool demeanor and his refusal to back down was beginning to bring out a darker force in Hayden.

"And what's stopping me from taking that gun from you?" he growled.

"The fact that I can use it to shoot you," Andrew replied coolly. Eliza barely recognized the man in front of her. The Andrew she knew was sweet, compromising, and enthusiastic. But *this* Andrew was cold, calculating, and stubborn as hell.

Hayden's eyes were taking on a menacing tinge, and Eliza observed as the hairs on his neck began to stand. *No, it can't be. He's not going to… or is he?*

"You say you can't trust him? How can we trust you? After the careless actions of your family, how can anybody in this town trust you?"

"Everything my family did, they did it to protect our town. They made tough decisions and they made sacrifices. I've been at odds with my family for many years, but when all is said and done, I acknowledge that everything they've done was for the greater good." Andrew was still looking straight ahead, his arm raised and steady. He seemed to be almost at ease, as if he had been training for this moment his entire life. Eliza wondered whether he'd really been at the bar all of the past Friday nights. Her whole image of Andrew was shattered and replaced by a new, more mysterious version of her boyfriend. She couldn't help but ache to know more about the man he really was.

But at this moment, the only important thing was her father's safety. She tried to look at Martin, but he was too far away for her to see his expression. Her father had lived through so many dangerous situations in his life; war, bombings, natural disasters… he had survived it all. Surely, he would survive this, too. *He can't die today. Martin always lives to tell the tale.*

Eliza unglued her eyes from Martin and looked at Hayden again. To her shock and anguish, there were more than a few hairs standing upright on his neck. In fact, Hayden was covered in hair. His already wide shoulders were expanding, bulging out of his shirt. His entire body was transforming at a rapid pace, and his destroyed clothes fell to the ground like limp rags. Hayden's form was menacing; he was still taller than Eliza, even when he stood on all fours. He uttered a growl through his sharp teeth, which forced Andrew to turn his head away from the other wolf. Just like Eliza, Andrew's face registered a look of shock. Hayden looked back at Andrew, his eyes ablaze. He emitted a low-pitched growl through sharp, clenched teeth.

Without thinking, Eliza ran to Andrew, shielding him with her body. However, to her surprise, Hayden wasn't charging toward Andrew. Instead, he was rapidly making his way toward the other wolf. Suddenly, the reality of what Hayden was doing dawned on her.

"Hayden, stop!" she yelled after him, but it was already too late. The other wolf released her father and was bounding toward Hayden, the two of them locking together in a death grip. They were snarling furiously at one another, and their movement was almost too fast for Eliza to keep up with. Martin was half running and half limping away from the scene, and Eliza ran toward him.

"Dad, are you hurt?"

Martin practically fell into her arms as she embraced him. His shoulder was bleeding profusely. Andrew ran over, ripping off his shirt and tearing off a shred. She wrapped it around the wound, pulling it tight. Martin didn't wince; he was no stranger to battle injuries. However, Eliza could tell that this was different. From the way her father swayed, she knew that he had lost a lot of blood. She and Andrew sat him down against a tree.

"Thank you, dear, I'm all right," Martin said softly, looking his daughter in the eyes. He looked proud.

Eliza held his hand and anxiously returned her gaze to the fight that was going on. Even though it was difficult to see what was happening, the sounds were highly audible. She flinched as she heard the sound of bodies hitting the ground, flesh tearing and teeth thrashing. For the first time in her life, Eliza found out what it was like to feel true fear. She knew that if the fight didn't stop soon, the werewolves would tear each other to death.

Entranced by the bloody spectacle, Eliza barely noticed the blur of a figure running across toward the wolves.

"Look!" Andrew yelled, pointing in the direction of the shape. Eliza strained her eyes; it looked like a regular man.

"Watch out!" she yelled toward him at the top of her lungs.

But it became clear that the man knew exactly where he was going. He was standing right by the scene of the fight, yelling up at the werewolves.

"Get away from there!" Andrew attempted, but without luck. The man persisted to shout.

Then, to their shock, the man did something unthinkable. He ran over and grabbed the other werewolf, holding on to him with all his might. It looked as if the man was trying to climb onto his back, but he wasn't actually moving. He just stood there and embraced the wolf.

The thrashing sounds stopped, and the wolf turned over to regard the man. Eliza prepared for the worst. She forced herself to stay alert, but every fiber of her body made her want to turn away. There was only one fate that could await this misguided stranger now…

A moment passed, and it felt as if time had stood still. Everyone braced for impact, but nothing else happened. The wolves weren't fighting anymore, and Hayden was slowly making his retreat. He was bleeding but not too intensely; the damage seemed manageable. By the time that Hayden reached Eliza, Andrew and Martin, he was back to his human form. Of course, he was completely naked, and Andrew threw the remainder of his shirt over to Hayden so he could cover up. Eliza had no words. She regarded Hayden as the hairs on his body grew back into his skin. It was an eerie but beautiful sight. To her surprise, Eliza could see the bruises and scars on his body begin to heal at an

unnaturally quick pace. His face was still, but his eyes
smiled back at her.

Eliza turned back to her father, tending to his
makeshift bandage and touching his head. Other than
the shoulder wound, his condition seemed to be fine.
She chatted to him and he chatted back, as if nothing
were the matter.

And then came the second gunshot of the night.
Eliza and Hayden spun around, taking in their
surroundings. Andrew was standing up, arms to the
side. He had a gun in his right arm, and it was smoking.
A loud cry of pure anguish emanated from the distance.
Eliza could see the shape of the other werewolf as he
lay on the ground. The man was standing over him,
weeping uncontrollably.

"What did you do?!" Hayden yelled at Andrew.

"I shot the thing that threatened my family."

"He was going away!" Hayden growled.

"He was a threat," Andrew responded calmly.

The sound of crying got louder and stronger from
the distance. The shape of the werewolf was still now,
unmoving.

"Those bullets… were they…?" Hayden asked
quietly.

"Yes. They were."

Hayden shook his head. "Goddamn you! You and your family, you're all the same. You don't care about anyone but yourselves."

"We do what needs to be done," Andrew replied calmly. He was still gripping his gun, and Eliza knew that he was prepared to use it on Hayden if he made a single move.

Eliza was beginning to make out some words in the distance as they mixed with the wails. She strained her ears to listen, and she thought that she had heard a sentence. *Is he saying what I think he's saying?*

Indeed, her senses weren't deceiving her. As the voice got louder, she could definitely hear the man saying, "I loved him! I loved him!"

As she listened to the sound of Jim wailing in the distance, Eliza bowed her head. She had known that Jim's lover was new in town and was working in the mines, but she hadn't put two and two together; she hadn't realized that he was a werewolf. And now, the only person Jim had ever loved was dead. She, on the other hand, had two men who loved her; one of them was a merciless killer and protector of men, while the other was a kind-hearted ferocious werewolf. *Boy, am I a lucky girl.*

-To be continued in Book 2-

If you enjoyed this title, I would appreciate your leaving a review of the book. Good reviews encourage an author to write as well as help books to sell. Good reviews can be just a few short sentences describing what you liked about the book without having a spoiler. If you could spend 30 seconds writing a review, I would appreciate it: you can review this title right now at your favorite retailer.

Here is a preview of the **next story** you may enjoy:

Alpha Feud: A BBW Paranormal Shifter Romance - Book 2

IT HAD been two days since Eliza's encounter with the supernatural. She still wasn't really sure what to think about everything she had witnessed. Not only did she have to deal with the fact that werewolves and God knows what else were real, but she also had to choose who to side with.

She had been with Andrew for so long. There was a history there. Did she really want to end a relationship of seven years for someone she had just met? But Hayden lit a fire inside of her that Andrew never had. She just wasn't sure if they had genuine feelings and chemistry or if it was just lust.

She had so much to think about and neither of them would leave her alone. They called and texted non-stop. She had asked Andrew to give her some time to think things through, so he went to stay with Tom and Brienne for a few days. Eliza was surprised that neither of the boys had tried coming to the house. Surprised and appreciative.

Eliza couldn't stop thinking about Jim and the pain he must be in over the loss of the love of his life. She would see him tomorrow at work, hopefully, and would be able see how he was doing. She wanted to ask him questions about werewolves, but now wasn't the right time. No matter how much alcohol Eliza fed the man, it wouldn't make it okay to drill him about his supernatural boyfriend.

Eliza glanced over at the end table beside the couch where her laptop was perched. She squinted her eyes and bit her bottom lip. *I could Google it.* She powered up her laptop. As she scrolled through hundreds of different websites, she realized that this really wasn't going to answer any of her questions. They were just stories and myths. How would she even know what was true?

Maybe I should just call Hayden. Eliza reached for her phone but didn't dial Hayden's number. She couldn't call Hayden. She was supposed to be trying to pick which guy she wanted. It would be too hard to focus on the pros and cons of each of them if she had one of them here with her to sway her vote.

She could call Hayden's brother, Theo. He would be able to tell her just as much as Hayden could. But then how would she explain to Melissa why she was calling her boyfriend to come over? *Maybe Melissa already knows what they are?* No, there was no way. She would have spilled the beans by now. If she called Theo, she was sure he would be able to come up with some excuse to keep Melissa from finding out.

Only problem was that she didn't have Theo's number. She couldn't ask Melissa for it, otherwise she would get suspicious and Eliza would be back to square one. She decided that she would text Hayden for Theo's number. There was no harm in that. If Hayden tried to talk to her about anything else, she would just tell him that she wasn't ready to discuss anything yet. She wouldn't be lying to him.

She picked up her phone again and found Hayden in her list of contacts. She sent a text asking him for Theo's number. She didn't have to wait long before her phone beeped. She wrote down the number Hayden had sent back, then thought about how she was going to answer the "why?" that had followed it. She decided it would be best to tell the truth. If she tried to lie to Hayden, he would probably pick up on it and come to the house.

She told him that she just had a few questions about werewolves, and she didn't want to have him come over to explain because she was still trying to figure out what her heart wanted and needed. Her finger hovered over the send button for a moment before she hit it. Once again, she didn't have to wait long for a reply. She was relieved when he said he understood.

She let out a long sigh and dialed Theo's number. He picked up on the second ring.

"Hello?" he answered casually.

"Theo? I need to ask you a favor." Eliza leaned against the headboard and closed her eyes.

"Sure. What do you need?" Theo's tone went from casual to serious.

"I just… I want to know more about you and Hayden. More about what you are." Eliza was still having trouble processing that they were not human and it sounded even more ridiculous when she said it out loud.

"Why not just ask Hayden?" he asked.

"I have other things going on in my head that involve Hayden and I don't want him to sway my decision." Eliza pushed herself from the bed and headed for the kitchen.

"Ah, I see." Eliza could almost hear his smile through the phone.

"So can you help me?" she asked again.

"Yes, I will swing by on my way to the mines. It'll be about half an hour. Is that all right?" Theo asked politely.

"Yes, that will be fine. Thank you." Eliza breathed out a sigh of relief.

"Okay see you then." Theo hung up the phone.

Eliza grabbed herself some toast and stood in the living room, watching out the window. She was finally going to get some answers. But what was she going to ask? She went into the kitchen and grabbed a pen and notepad. She spent the half hour waiting for Theo by jotting down some questions.

If you enjoyed this sample then look for **Alpha Feud: A BBW Paranormal Shifter Romance - Book 2.**

Here is a preview of **another story** you may also enjoy:

Romeo Alpha: A BBW Paranormal Shifter Romance - Book 1

AMANDA WONDERED how the hell she had gotten so far away from home. When she walked, she usually didn't go past a couple of blocks, but she felt so different today. Something was pushing her further and in a different direction, and she wasn't sure what it was. But she didn't care at the moment, because she just wanted to walk.

Not thinking twice about where she was going, she let her gut instinct give her the direction she needed.

Her grandmother had always told her to go with her gut. She'd said human instinct was better than anything. "Intuition is a girl's best friend," she would say, and then they would both laugh. Talks she and her grandmother had always seemed to pop into her head at the strangest of times, like now.

Here she was, going for a walk, and wondering why she wanted to go in a different direction, and there was her grandmother's voice in her head, propelling her along. Amanda missed her grandmother more with every passing year.

Amanda paused and thought about her life thus far. She had just graduated from college and started working in the local animal hospital, but it wasn't quite like she had thought. She didn't see the care and passion she'd hoped to find in the industry. In the city, being a vet was all about how much money you could make, how many pets you could treat. And, at twenty-four, it was hard to be taken seriously.

Her two female roommates were nice, but they all just went their separate ways. They didn't eat ice cream and watch movies like on *Friends*. They didn't share secrets or even laugh or hang out. They really just slept in the same apartment, and they usually weren't even home at the same time. Except Amanda, that is.

Amanda was always at home, it seemed. She had nowhere else to go, really. The other two girls spent most nights out with their real friends or their boyfriends. Amanda lived a lonely life, but she was happy. At least, she was pretty sure she was happy. After all, she had an upstanding career, and she still had money left over from her savings.

Both her parents had been killed in a car accident years ago. Amanda had graduated from high school with no family there that day or on the day she graduated from college. It was what it was, though, and she knew that her parents watched her from Heaven.

The only positive thing was that her parents had been prepared and had made sure they left enough money and a big enough life insurance policy to help her out. They would be surprised but happy knowing how much that money had helped her in the years after their death. She was proud to say that she was able to live off of it through her college years. She'd never even had to get a job like most kids did. Amanda had been able to focus on her classes.

That freedom wasn't worth it, though. She would have worked three jobs at a time while going to school for one more day with her parents.

However, the account was finally starting to dry up, and she needed to think about what she would do. Sure, she had a new job that could pay her bills, but those loans were piling up with interest. Even a vet job only went so far.

Amanda sighed as she began the trek back toward the house.

Amanda liked her walks in the evening. It helped her to relax, enjoying the quiet time alone. And while Amanda wasn't overweight by any means, it helped slim her waistline, which showed those extra biscuits she liked every now and again.

She turned and began to make her way back to the townhouse she shared with her roommates, but stopped as she heard a noise

A rustling came from behind her, and she turned to see the bushes shaking. Looking over to the other side of the sidewalk, she saw those bushes shake as well. Not wanting to wait around to find out what was behind the leaves, she took off at a run. She swore she heard a growl come from behind her, but she didn't turn to see what was chasing her. That would only slow her down. As she reached the door to her home, she quickly turned the knob and went through headfirst. Shutting the door quickly, she looked out the window. She got a glimpse of a long black furry tail as something ran around to the side of her building.

"What in the world are you doing, Amanda?" Betsy stood there looking at her inquisitively.

"Something was chasing me."

"What?"

"I don't know what it was, but something big and furry was chasing me. I saw a long black tail just now when I walked into the house."

"You mean when you dove into the house?" Betsy's grin faded. "I'll call the game warden. If there is a big animal outside, then none of us need to go out there until they find it and get rid of it."

"Well, I don't want them to kill it."

"I know, silly, but if it's a wild animal, they can take it out to the National Forest and let it loose. The city is no place for a wild animal." Betsy turned and picked up the phone from the receiver.

Amanda stood in shocked silence as she listened to her roommate tell the person on the other end of the phone what had happened.

She knew from Betsy's tone that she and the person on the other end of the phone were questioning her sanity. They lived in a big city, and the closest thing they got to a wild animal was a stray cat or two. They didn't even get raccoons. If there was some huge animal like she thought, then it would make headline news.

Shaking her head in aggravation, Amanda turned toward her room. She suddenly felt silly and didn't want to have to explain what she saw to any more people.

"Amanda? Where are you going? They are on their way and might need to talk to you."

"Tell them it was a dog. Now that I'm thinking about it, it kind of looked like that couple that lives down the road's greyhound. Maybe he just got out."

"Are you sure, Amanda?" Betsy asked, turning and saying something into the phone.

Without saying another word, Amanda shut the door to her room tight and then quickly locked the door. She looked over her room and, seeing the window open and the curtains blowing in the breeze, she ran over to push the window pane down and lock it tight. As she stood there, she looked out into the woods that made up her backyard. There, in the distance, two yellow eyes stared back at her.

Suddenly, more eyes appeared, and it seemed the animals went on forever. She was amazed, since the woods behind her house were very dense and small. The dark night was lit with a full moon. A shiver raced through her as she stood there and stared into the first set of yellow eyes. She quickly shut the curtains and went to sit on her bed. She didn't think she would ever be able to fall asleep knowing what was out there. As she laid her head on the pillow, her mind wondered to large beasts with yellow eyes and sharp fangs. But she was soon fast asleep.

<<<>>>

Amanda awoke with a yawn. It had been almost a month since the incident with what she now called a dog. She had agreed with Betsy that her mind had been playing tricks on her that night. There were often times when she was sure she felt eyes on her, and she would turn in one direction or another, looking. What she was seeking, she didn't know, but somewhere in the back of her mind, she just wanted to know if the eyes she had seen that night had been real or just part of her dreams that evening. She was still so uneasy about it that her walks seemed to get earlier and earlier each evening.

She was just about to walk out the door when her phone started ringing. She quickly grabbed it and pushed the button to answer it.

"Hello."

"Ms. Walker?"

"Yes?"

"Hello, Ms. Walker, my name is Ernest Montgomery. I am calling to tell you that your aunt has passed away."

"My aunt? But I don't have any family. You must have the wrong Ms. Walker."

"No, ma'am. Your father was Joshua Walker, correct? Mother Maureen Walker?"

"Yes."

"Then, I have the right Ms. Walker. It is your father's sister I am referring to. She unexpectedly passed away from a heart attack. I am very sorry for your loss."

"Oh, my gosh! I never knew I even had any family. I am very sad that I didn't get to meet her."

"Yes, ma'am. I'm sure. She was a nice woman. I have also called you to see if you can meet with me. I need to go over her will with you."

"Her will?"

"Yes, ma'am. Your aunt was a wealthy woman."

"Oh? Um, okay. When would you like to meet?"

"The sooner, the better."

"Okay. How about today?"

"That would be great. I am in Slatesville, in the valley. "

"Oh. Okay. That is just forty-five minutes from me. I can be there in a couple of hours."

"Sounds good, ma'am. I am at the *Montgomery Law Firm*. I am the only attorney in the town."

"Okay. Thank you, sir. I will see you soon."

"Yes, ma'am. I'll be waiting."

Amanda fell back on the couch, stunned, for what seemed like forever. Everything was pushed to the back of her mind as she thought about what she had just learned. She had a family. Well, she *did* have a family. Now her aunt was gone. Could there be others in her family who she knew nothing about? She didn't know, but she did know one thing. She wasn't going to find out sitting around here, twiddling her thumbs. She needed to get going fast.

Amanda headed for the kitchen. She wasn't surprised to see that no one was there. Of course her roommates weren't home. They were either in class or with their boyfriends.

Smiling, she made a cup of coffee and drank it slowly, thinking about what she might find out. Then, with a deep sigh, she made her way to her car. She looked at the small Honda with pride. It was a pile of junk to some, but it held a special place in her heart. She hadn't been able to get rid of her father's car. Instead, she had sold her own.

She looked down at the small picture he had taped to the dash near the speedometer. She was about six in the picture, and she had been holding her mom's cheeks in her hands as she kissed her.

She remembered the day like it was yesterday. They had just got to a cabin they vacationed in. She had enjoyed herself so much. The little cabin had one bedroom with a queen-sized bed where her parents slept and a set of bunk beds for her. They had stayed up late roasting marshmallows as her father told her scary stories about wolves and vampires. She had ended up in their bed, snuggled between the two of them. They had spent the next day hiking and walking trails and seeing tons of waterfalls and animals.

She had loved it and had never forgotten. It soon became a family tradition to go camping every year. After some of those trips, they didn't return home.

Instead, they moved on to a different location. The constant moving had been hard on her as a kid, but she would have never told her parents that. She had felt like they were hiding something from her. Of course, she had been young back then and had blown it off as childhood curiosity. Now, with this new family member, she wasn't so sure.

Her parents had been very quiet people. They seemed cautious of everything going on around them and were even a little jumpy at times. Maybe there was more going on here than she thought. She needed to find out.

She wiped away a tear and go in the car. The car had a huge dent in one side and was almost fifteen years old, but it got her where she needed to go. She slid the car into drive and smiled to herself.

"Dad would be proud that his car was still running so good, wouldn't he, Trixy?" She and her father had named the car together.

Amanda turned onto the next road and made her way down the narrow two-lane road that led into the mountains. She had never been this way because her parents always went the long way around the mountains. They said they liked to take the scenic route.

She came to a small wooden sign that said *Slatesville—Welcome to your home away from home*. She smiled at the welcoming sign and kept on her way to the town. As she drove, she was amazed at how beautiful everything was. The low-hanging branches of the trees scraped the roof of the car every once in a while.

She was amazed at how many animals she saw. Deer acted as if they weren't afraid of her car. Raccoons were plentiful, and she jumped when a large black snake slithered across the road. There were people all around, and they watched her car curiously as she made her way down the street.

The town reminded her of a long lost western ghost town. It was a little spooky, and she caught herself checking the doors to make sure they were locked. The men nodded at her as she moved forward and many of the people smiled, although they held themselves back a little.

Amanda finally saw the sign that said *Montgomery Law Firm*. She pulled into one of the many vacant parking spots and slowly got out of the car. A handsome man leaned against the building she was about to enter. His brown eyes had flecks of yellow and orange in their deep depths. She smiled slightly, and the man just continued to stare as he looked her over slowly.

"Can I help you, ma'am?"

"I am just here to see Mr. Montgomery."

"Well, you're in the right place, Miss…?"

"Oh, Amanda. Amanda Walker. And you are?"

Something changed in his eyes as he smiled at her and made his way to her side. He held out his hand to her. "Name's Curtis Livingston."

"Oh. Do you live here?"

"Yes. I'm one of the controlling partners here in Slatesville. Well, I have to be going. It was good to meet you."

"You, too, Mr. Livingston."

"Please, call me Curt. Everyone does."

"Only if you call me Amanda."

"That's a deal, sweet lady." She flushed all over when he raised her hand to his lips and gently caressed her knuckles with a brief touch of his mouth. She felt the rise in temperature in her cheeks spread across her upper chest. She stood there and watched as he walked away from her down the street to slip inside a store. She felt foolish and realized that she had been staring. She shook her head, trying to think straight and clear the thoughts that were running through her mind.

Amanda was always aware that she wasn't the Barbie doll type of girl. Although she wasn't fat, she wasn't rail thin, which most men liked, either. Her waist and stomach didn't look like a washboard, although it didn't look like a bunch of bread dough either.

She instantly felt inadequate and quickly turned around to walk to the door of the attorney's office. Knocking, she was surprised when the door instantly opened. The man who opened the door wasn't what she expected. Mr. Montgomery was a short, pudgy man. He didn't wear a business suit, and he didn't seem stuffy at all. He was older and had a short goatee around his mouth. His hair was pulled back into a ponytail at the back of his neck, and he smiled when he saw her.

"You must be Amanda. You look just like your father, except for your eyes. You have your mother's eyes. Let's hope you didn't inherit your father's temper, though," he chuckled.

"You knew my father?"

"Oh, why yes, my dear. We grew up together, Josh and I. Have to say we got into a lot of trouble as kids, and your aunt Mabel was always there to wag her finger and tell on us. You see, there were the three of us; Joshua, Jeremiah, and I. We were called the three musketeers. Mabel wanted to be the fourth, but you know boys. We would never let her, so she always ran and told on us to get back at us for not including her; the little minx." He told the story fondly, and she instantly knew that this man held her family in the highest regard. She also knew he was her ticket to finding out the truth about her family.

"Do I have any more family that I don't know of?" She held her breath, as though she were a child again, asking if Santa Claus was real.

"I am sure you do, my dear. Unfortunately, your aunt was the last of your father's line. She couldn't have any children, and most of the family was killed in a fire in '90. I am sure there is still family on your mother's side, though. However, I must warn you that they are not the kind of people you want to know. Now, if you will come in, I will tell you about everything that now belongs to you."

"What?"

"Oh, my dear, you must know that your father's family had a legacy. You are the only Traverse left to take over the family business."

"What? I don't know what you're talking about."

"They never did tell you who you really are, did they? Oh, you poor child. I am afraid you are going to learn some things about yourself that are going to be hard for you. You must still be a virgin as well."

"I beg your pardon, sir, but I don't see how that's any of your damn business."

"No, my dear, I do not mean to be crude. I was just saying that you have never undergone the Change. It will happen, though. You recently turned twenty-four, and everything changes now."

"What change? What in the hell are you talking about?"

"They hid that from you, too? Oh my gosh. You don't know? Oh, Lord. Okay, first things first. You are now the owner of your family's estate."

"Family estate? So I have a house."

He smiled kindly at her. "Not just a house, my dear. It is what holds the legacy of your family name together. The estate has fifteen bedrooms with their own bathrooms and fireplaces, a kitchen, dining room, parlor, living area, office, library, Carolina room, staff quarters, wrap-around porch with two different sections screened in, pool, tennis courts and 300 acres. It was the pride and joy of your ancestor, Edgar. He was a distant grandfather of yours."

"Oh my gosh."

"Yes, ma'am. How about this? How about I get the keys and directions to the place? You go take a look at it, and then we can talk tomorrow about what you want to do. Stephan has been looking over things, and since your aunt's death, he has given everyone time off until you arrive and decide where to go from there."

Amanda wasn't sure she had the energy to deal with all of this tonight. "Unfortunately, it is very late. Is there somewhere that I can stay for a couple days and then I can go from there and take the day tomorrow to go look at the place?"

"That is perfect. Just give me a second, and I'll find a place for you to stay tonight."

Amanda sat quietly and listened to him talk on his phone. She didn't even hear his words as she thought of what she was going to do.

"I have gotten you a little cabin to rent down the road," he said, drawing her attention back to him. "It is in the woods a little but has electricity and such. On such short notice, I couldn't find anything else. It is only about ten minutes away. The key will be under the mat at the front door. Just go on in and make yourself at home."

"That is perfect. Thank you so much."

"You're welcome, my dear, and we will talk tomorrow. Say ten o'clock tomorrow morning? We will meet here and go to see the house together."

"Perfect. Thank you, Mr. Montgomery."

If you enjoyed this sample then look for **Romeo Alpha: A BBW Paranormal Shifter Romance - Book 1.**

Here is a preview of **another story** you may also enjoy:

**Fifty Recipes For Disaster: A New Adult Romance
Series - Book 1 by Carla Coxwell**

"**ALL RIGHT**, chefs, you have ninety seconds to get
your food plated and presented. If your dish isn't ready,
you will automatically be eliminated."

My cooking instructor, Chef Michelle Lee, walks
through the room, examining our stations. My fellow
cooking students and I are competing for the chance to
enter another competition. The winner of today's
cooking challenge will get the chance to compete for a
full-time apprenticeship at Fission, one of Austin's
hottest restaurants.

I'm not confident in many aspects of my life, but I
know I dominate in the kitchen. I begin plating my dish
just as Chef Lee approaches my station.

"Your food presents beautifully as usual, Kiara,"
she tells me with a smile. "If it tastes as good as it
looks, you've got this in the bag," she adds with a soft
whisper.

The instructors at *Le Cordon Bleu College of
Culinary Arts* aren't supposed to show favoritism to
their students, but Chef Lee keeps a soft spot for me.
Along with being one of my teachers, she's also my
faculty adviser, and she knows the unusual
circumstances that brought me to the school.

"Time's up," she calls out to the class. "Place your
finished plates on the head table."

I walk my plate to the front of the room and place it on top of the placard that holds my student ID number. My classmates follow suit… several of them glare at me after looking at my dish. I am delighted, knowing they're all both jealous and impressed I was able to execute a well-developed *Cioppino* within the given time frame. My rich seafood stew is accompanied by fresh sourdough loaves. I examine my classmates' dishes and feel my chances of winning are good.

"Clear away your stations," Chef Lee directs. "Chef Lawton will be here shortly to judge your plates, and I don't want any evidence of who made what on display when he arrives."

Chef Lawton is the *sous* chef at Fission and the judge of this stage of the apprenticeship competition. I clear my station quickly and then I take a seat at the front of the room. I want to be able to see Chef Lawton's expressions as he tastes each dish.

As I sit nervously in my chair, my classmates finish clearing their stations. I can tell everyone else is just as anxious as I am… we've received plenty of critiques from our instructors but this will be the first time a professional chef from a restaurant will be tasting our food. The door of the classroom opens and a tall man wearing a black chef's jacket enters the room.

"Chef Lawton, it's so lovely to see you," Chef Lee welcomes him. "I can't tell you how excited we are to participate in this competition."

"We're excited as well," Chef Lawton replies. "We're always looking for new, innovative chefs at

Fission. I'm looking forward to tasting the dishes and welcoming one of your students into the final leg of the competition. I see that all of the plates are ready. If it's all right with you, I'll get started."

"Of course," Chef Lee agrees.

I try not to hold my breath as I watch Chef Lawton sample each of the plates. I feel encouraged when he reaches mine. Instead of sampling one bite and moving on, he holds the broth in his mouth for a moment, and then tastes each type of seafood in turn. The expression on his face tells me that my stew is perfect, and I say a silent prayer I haven't been out-cooked by any of my classmates.

"First off, I'd like to say this is an impressive display," the seasoned chef begins. "Everything on this table is up to par with the level of skill and talent I expect to see from second-year students. That being said, there is a clear winner. One chef not only executed a delicious dish, but also added a few subtle, original touches that showed innovation and creativity."

Adrenaline rushes through me as he moves to stand behind my dish. "Who created this *Cioppino*?" he asks.

I blush involuntarily as I raise my hand.

"And what is your name, Chef?"

"Kiara Sands," I reply, trying to mask the excitement in my voice.

"Well, Chef Sands, it's an honor to welcome you to the next stage of the competition. I look forward to tasting more of your food as the weeks progress. I am needed back at Fission, but Chef Lee will provide you with the details of your new position." He turns to the rest of the class. "To the rest of you, don't be discouraged. You all provided me with excellent dishes, and you have bright futures ahead of you."

"Thank you, Chef," the class responds in unison.

Chef Lawton makes a quick exit, and Chef Lee takes his place behind the head table. "Excellent work today, class. You're dismissed until tomorrow," she announces. My classmates gather their things and leave the room… I stay behind to talk to Chef Lee.

"Kiara, I'm so proud of you." She beams once we are alone. "As you know, there will be two other chefs competing with you at Fission. You're the only one who's been selected from *Le Cordon Bleu*, and I know you'll represent us well." She moves to her desk and pulls a large package from her bottom drawer. "Here is your apprenticeship packet. You'll receive your Fission jacket when you report for work tomorrow morning. If you have any questions, or just need someone to talk to, you know where to reach me."

"This seems like a wonderful dream, and part of me is afraid that I'll wake up any minute now," I confess.

Chef Lee gives me a maternal smile. "This is a dream, Kiara. It's *your* dream. And you're well on your way to achieving it."

The information packet Chef Lee presented me with instructs me to be at Fission at 10:00 am. I check my dashboard clock as I pull into the parking lot… 9:40 am. I feel smug, knowing I'm probably the first of the three competitors to arrive. I check my makeup in the rear-view mirror before exiting my car.

Fission is housed in a modern brick building in East Austin, one of the city's burgeoning hipster areas. The area gives off a relaxed, laid-back vibe, but I know the kitchen of Fission will be anything but.

I push open the heavy, solid oak door and am greeted by a pixy-sized hostess with spiked, lavender hair.

"Table for one?" she asks me brightly.

"No," I reply nervously. "My name is Kiara Sands. I'm supposed to start work today."

"Oh! You're one of the newbies!" She says warmly. "I'm Megan. It's a pleasure to meet you. The other two are already here. I'll show you to their table."

Damn it! I'd been so sure I'd make the best impression by arriving first, and here I am, the last of the apprentices to report for our first day.

Megan seems to sense my disappointment. "Don't worry. Paul doesn't give a shit how early people show up. As long as you're here when you're scheduled, you'll be fine. And you haven't missed anything. The other two have just been sitting alone since they got here," she offers reassuringly.

"Thank you for that," I say half-heartedly. As I follow Megan through the restaurant, I'm struck by the eclectic, well-placed décor. All of the tables are made of the same polished oak as the front door. The water goblets on the tabletops are tinted in hues of blue, green, and rose… a selection of art from all around the world adorns the walls. The ambiance is on the right side of the fine line between cozy and overwhelming. The restaurant offers a large main dining room, with smaller, more private rooms on each side.

"This is a beautiful place," I say as Megan leads me toward the back of the main room.

"It is," she agrees. "Paul handled all of the decorating himself. He says that Austin is a melting pot, and he wants all of our customers to feel at home when they dine here."

I'm about to comment on how successfully that goal had been achieved when we arrive at a table occupied by a beautiful blonde woman and a swarthy man with sandy blond hair. A pot of coffee and three cups sit on the table.

"Kiara Sands, this is Jenny Foster and Robbs Martin," Megan introduces us. She checks her watch before speaking again. "It's a quarter to ten, so I imagine that Paul will be out shortly. I suggest you get fully caffeinated and enjoy this time off your feet. It will be the last one for today," she warns with a friendly, knowing tone.

I take a seat in the chair next to Jenny as Megan moves back to the hostess station. "It's a pleasure to meet you both," I offer.

"It's a pleasure to meet you too," Robbs replies. "Congratulations on making it this far in the competition. And I'd like to apologize right now for how thoroughly I'm going to kick both of your asses. This job is mine." He speaks with a blend of arrogance and sarcasm, and I can tell immediately that Robbs and I are not going to get along.

Personal relationships are something I struggle with. In my experience, there's no point in getting close to someone who will inevitably let you down. I prefer to keep my head down and focus on getting my job done. As Chef Lee said yesterday, I have a dream and I'm well on my way to achieving it. I'll be damned if I let Robbs or anyone else get in my way.

"Just ignore Robbs," Jenny advises me. "He thinks that he's God's gift to food... women too, probably." She giggles. "So Kiara, what's your story? Which campus were you plucked from?"

"I'm in my second year at *Le Cordon Bleu*," I answer with pride. In my opinion, *Le Cordon Bleu* is the best culinary school in the area—it's also the hardest to get in to. Jenny seems impressed by my background, but Robbs laughs and dismisses it immediately.

"The *Bleu* is all right, I guess," he snorts, "if you're happy being complacent and doing everything old-school."

"I wasn't aware that being classically trained is a bad thing," I reply shortly. "Tell me, what culinary Mecca do you hail from?"

"*Escoffier*," he answers with a cocky smile. "You know, where all of the innovative, cutting-edge people attend. Three of my instructors were nominated for the James Beard award. So like I said, no hard feelings, but I'm going to kick both of your asses. *Escoffier* specializes in farm-to-table cuisine, so I'm exactly the kind of chef Fission is looking for."

I dismiss his statement with a glare. While the *Auguste Escoffier School of Culinary Arts* is reputed for turning out fantastic chefs, in some culinary circles it's dismissed as a hipster college that prioritizes food trends over basic technique and skill.

I don't feel like debating the merits of my education with Robbs, so I turn to Jenny. "And where do you go?" I ask pleasantly.

"The Art Institute," she replies. "I'm still not positive that cooking is my life's passion. I wanted to go to a college that offers other programs, in case I decided to change my major."

"If you're not sure that you want to be a chef, then what the fuck are you doing here?" Robbs asks hotly. "You should give your spot to someone who knows that this is what they want."

Jenny's green eyes fill with both anger and embarrassment, and I can tell she's fumbling for a response.

"I don't agree with that at all," I say warmly. "What better way to find out if you enjoy working in a real kitchen, than by actually doing it?"

"That's exactly what my instructor said when I won this spot," Jenny says with a nod.

"I see how it's going to be," Robbs interjects with more sarcasm. "The two of you are going to band together in 'sisterhood' and gang up on me."

"That's not how it's going to be at all," a firm voice says from behind me. I turn to see one of the most attractive men I've ever laid my eyes on. He's tall, with broad shoulders, blue eyes, and sandy blond hair. He's also wearing a black chef's jacket, identical to the one Chef Lawton wore when he judged my dish. He holds eye contact with me for several moments before he speaks again.

"This competition will come down to one thing and one thing only... the quality of your food. Only one of you will be named my new apprentice, so ganging up on each other won't serve any purpose. I'm Paul Weston, and I'd like to welcome you to my restaurant." He extends his hand to me.

I respond with a firm handshake and a smile. "I'm Kiara Sands. Thank you for this opportunity."

"You're here because you deserve to be. No thanks are necessary," he assures me.

If you enjoyed this sample then look for **Fifty Recipes For Disaster: A New Adult Romance Series - Book 1 by Carla Coxwell**.

Other Books by Darla Dunbar

- The Romeo Alpha BBW Paranormal Shifter Romance Series

- Romeo Alpha Blood Lines Romance Series

- The Alpha Packed BBW Paranormal Shifter Romance Series

- The Daemon Paranormal Romance Chronicles

- The Mind Talker Paranormal Romance Series

- The Leather Satchel Paranormal Romance Series

Get the latest update on new releases from the author at:

https://darladunbar.com/newsletter/

About the Author - Darla Dunbar

Darla has been interested in paranormal romance since she was a teenager in high school. It was then that she discovered she could fulfill her fantasies through her writing.

Observing people and human behavior in the area of romance has always been one of her favorite pastimes. Combining that with an overactive imagination is a sure fire way of coming up with interesting themes.

Connect with Darla Dunbar

I really appreciate you reading my book! Here are my social media coordinates:

Friend me on Facebook:
https://www.facebook.com/darladunbar/

Follow me on Twitter: https://twitter.com/DarlDunbar

Check me out on Goodreads:
https://www.goodreads.com/author/show/8425857.Darl a_Dunbar

Subscribe to my newsletter:
https://darladunbar.com/newsletter/

Visit my website: https://darladunbar.com/